Fables from Old French:
Aesop's Beasta and Bumpkins

Fables from
Old French

Fables from Old French

Aesop's Beasts and Bumpkins

Translated by
NORMAN R. SHAPIRO

Introduction by
HOWARD NEEDLER

WESLEYAN UNIVERSITY PRESS
Middletown, Connecticut

Translation © 1982 by Norman R. Shapiro

Introduction © 1982 by Howard Needler

Published by Wesleyan University Press, 110 Mt. Vernon Street
Middletown, Connecticut 06457

Distributed by Harper & Row, Publishers,
Keystone Industrial Park
Scranton, Pennsylvania 18512

Woodcuts from *Les Subtiles Fables D'Esope* (Lyon: Mathieu
Husz, 1484; reprint edited by Claude Dalbanne and E. Droz,
Lyon: Association Guillaume Le Roy, 1926). Reproduced with
permission of the New York Public Library.

*Illustrations on the title page and on pages 19, 23, 27, 31, 39, 43, and 133 were
adapted by Joyce Kachergis.*

Book design by Joyce Kachergis

LIBRARY OF CONGRESS CATALOGING IN PUBLICATION DATA

Aesop's Fables.
  Fables from Old French.

  1. French poetry—To 1500—Translations into English.
2. French poetry—To 1500.   3. Fables, French—Transla-
tions into English.   4. Fables, French.   5. English
poetry—Translations from French.   6. Fables, English
—Translations from French.   I. Shapiro, Norman R.
II. Needler, Howard.   III. Title.
PQ1308.E4A47   1982   841'.1'08   82–17384
ISBN 0–8195–5074–4

Manufactured in the United States of America
First Edition

Contents

Translator's Preface

Aesthetic labels—the names so many literary types like to pin on works in the game of categorization—tend to come in opposing pairs. We weigh works for their dosages of the classic and romantic, the realistic and fantastic, the tragic and comic—*j'en passe, et des meilleurs*—and come up with an appropriate assay that satisfies our need to "get a handle" on them, or, with a more etymologically orthodox synonym, to "comprehend" them. To label a work is, in a sense, to possess it.

One of the particularly time-honored oppositions is the didactic/artistic. The terms are, of course, relative, since I daresay there is almost no literature that can't be accused of teaching somebody something—of suggesting ideas, shaping tastes, refining conceptions—however little that may be its author's purpose. Even the most avowedly non-didactic examples of art-for-art's-sake carry an implied message: that of artistic validity without fore- or afterthought. But the dichotomy is useful all the same in a general consideration of an author's intent, and its result. Few, I think, will argue with the assertion that the "morals" of Musset's *proverbes*, for example, are far less important than their artistry; or, to take another theatrical example, that the social messages of the dramas of Dumas *fils* far outweigh their aesthetic worth. At the midpoint of the scale, to cite an example closer to the present texts, if La Fontaine is immortal today, it is both for the didactic lessons imparted to generations of artistically unsophisticated French children, and for the sophistication, the craft, the wit—in short, the artistry—of his verse.

The originals of the medieval fables here translated are more difficult to assess in this regard. By the very nature of the beast, it is not always easy to appreciate the artistic intent or the resulting artistic merit of authors whose language does not yield up its nuances as readily as varieties closer to our own time. Medievalists are generally much less aesthetically demanding than their modernist colleagues. The mere physical existence of a manuscript, like a piece of the True Cross—its escape unscathed from the floods, wars, monastery burnings, and other less dramatic, everyday ravages of time—is cause for rejoicing and sufficient reason for a philologically critical edition by an aspiring doctoral candidate, at the very least. And understandably so. Aesthetic canons change with time. Do we judge medieval works by contemporary standards (when we can deduce them) or by our own? Assuming that we can resolve that problem, can we penetrate the linguistic barriers well enough to be truly competent judges? Can we tell with any certainty, for instance, what was intended as high seriousness and what was sarcasm? Can we presume to know all the overtones and undertones of words and idioms that are often attested in only a few examples, and sometimes in no more than one? Can we, in short, offer more in an aesthetic judgment of many medieval texts than educated guesses? Paradoxically, we are usually more comfortable, in this regard, with the more remote works of Classical Antiquity than with much of the literature of the Middle Ages.

However, if the artistic element of many medieval texts is debatable, the didactic element in the moralistic works that abound is always quite clear, especially in the fables. So clear, in fact that in two of the collections represented here, the *moralité* is unerringly and explicitly announced as such, lest there be any doubt. As a result, the translator feels little compunction about attacking such texts. The artistic *per se* being hardly an issue, there is less inherently untranslatable in them, and he is less likely, therefore, to do them obvious violence. In other words, he can be a *traduttore* without (at least apparently) being an aesthetic *traditore*. Perhaps this is one of the attractions I find in translating medieval verse. There is relatively little risk of being raked over the critical coals for wantonly committing aesthetic mayhem. As long as he transmits the message as faithfully as frequent ambiguities and obscurities allow, and as long as he gives something of the flavor of the originals—the form, the rhymes, the rhythms—the translator enjoys a comfortable latitude. The artistic results will depend more on his own particular talents than on those of the original poet. And while he may not necessarily write a "good" translation, it will not, at least, be a "wrong" one.

The present translations, written sporadically over a number of years, reflect the liberties suggested in the foregoing remarks. Here and there I have added bits of interpretation to fill out problematic passages, or chosen to see humor where the medieval author may—or, then again, may not—have been in deadly earnest. On the technical side, I have often played with alliterations and internal rhymes even where none may exist in the original. Anyone looking for literal translations had best leave these aside, as should anyone who feels that a translation should be written in the idiosyncratic idiom of its own day, whatever the period of the work itself. Many modern translators—the late Paul Blackburn comes immediately to mind—argue that, if the medieval poet was writing in the language of his time, we can only be faithful to him by writing in the language of ours. The argument, however, logical as it is, has somehow never convinced me. For me, a translation of medieval verse needs enough formal structure and enough linguistic distance—not archaism, which is itself a kind of artificiality—to maintain an antique tone. When put into free verse, or into colloquial American English, no matter how skillfully, it ceases to be a medieval poem—an adaptation, yes, but not a translation. Analogously, Anouilh's *Antigone* and Cocteau's *La Machine infernale* are virtuoso renditions of classical themes, but neither playwright claimed to have "translated" Sophocles.

I hope my readers will share my philosophy. For those who do not, there still remains the pleasure of reading Howard Needler's elegant and erudite introduction. I thank him not only for providing my translations with such a substantial scholarly underpinning, but also for participating so energetically in the entire enterprise.

My thanks also to James Wadsworth, professor, collaborator, and friend, for fostering my interest in things medieval; to Robert Rainwater, Keeper of Prints, New York Public Library, for his courteous assistance; to Sleeth Mitchell, of Inkling Press, whose elegant chapbook editions of "The Peasant and the Beetle" and "The Ass That Played the Hound" have already become collector's items; to Angel Flores and Elizabeth Dulaney, for their kind interest in my work; to Wesleyan University, generous in its support; and to the friends— Caldwell Titcomb, Evelyn Simha, Lillian Bulwa, and so many more—who have patiently listened. Most especially, my thanks to my father, for his encouragement, and to the memory of my mother, whose love of poetry and way with words taught me more than all the books.

—NORMAN R. SHAPIRO

Cambridge, Massachusetts

Introduction

I

The animal fable has been dear to the human race for a very long time, and is found in virtually all cultures.[1] Particular motifs, and even character types and plots, have occurred in widely separated times and places, and although such correspondence has given rise to various interpretations, one thing it clearly suggests is a universal interest in the application of animal lore to the human condition. A capacity to see animals and their behavior in anthropomorphic guise is prerequisite to the making of animal fables. Some ancient artifacts show that people already thought in this way over four thousand years ago. A charming example is an Early Dynastic inlaid harp soundbox from Ur.[2] Its human-headed bulls and scorpion-man display a conjunction of animal and human that will probably remain permanently mysterious to us. But the soundbox also displays animal servants and musicians, a different duality whose human functions in animal guise can delight, amuse, and, if we knew their story, instruct. Henri Frankfort is probably right to suggest that works of art such as this harp soundbox conveyed in their designs more than "mere fables."[3] Nonetheless, their representational forms, whether directed to religious and other more solemn ends, or to play, are analogous to those of fable.

In answer to the question, "What is a fable?" Ben Edwin Perry quotes the four-word definition of the rhetorician Theon: *logos pseudes eikonizon aletheian*, which he translates as "a fictitious story picturing a truth."[4] The first two words of this phrase address the narrative and fictive character of almost all fables; the last two suggest, as Perry notes, that fable is something like metaphor, clothing an idea in a form of words that give it force, color and appeal. The definition as a whole implies that fable enlists fiction in the cause of truth. This view places fable among the stock-in-trade of the ancient orator: Perry notes such rhetorical use of Greek prose fables.[5] (The form made a difference: Greek or Latin fables written in verse could be regarded as literature, a category from which prose fables were excluded.) The Roman poet Phaedrus offers his own explanation of the origin of fable:

> Now I will explain briefly why the type of thing called fable was invented. The slave, being liable to punishment for any offence, since he dared not say outright what he wished to say, projected his personal sentiments into fables and eluded censure under the guise of jesting with made-up stories.[6]

This notion that fable was invented by slaves, a product of the experience of enslavement, seems connected with motifs in the biography of Aesop, who enters history as a black slave. At the same time, Phaedrus is making a covert allusion to the poetic fictions of all poets. Fables, even if they say only what everybody knows and readily acknowledges to be true, say what those in power prefer not to hear.

The typical content of fables is the presentation of human and animal behavior with more or less satirical commentary, occasionally allied to moral or ethical teaching. There is nothing in this to deny a literary form of composition, but fables also incorporate so much popular wisdom and folklore as to suggest that they existed and were transmitted by word of mouth long before they were written down in verse or prose. Some fables seem to consist of nothing more than the amplification of a proverb: in such cases the fable may look as if it was made to suggest the "origin" of the proverb, or to exemplify its idea—or it may constitute an imaginative elaboration of the proverb's condensed verbal statement. In this respect fables may seem tangent with the forms called *mashal* in Hebrew, and in Arabic, *mathal*.[7] These words allude to pithy aphorism more than anything else; its similarity to the Aesopic fable resides in the latter's "metaphoric" character, and shows another way to understand it. As the *mashal* or *mathal* makes a general statement susceptible of specific application, the fable may say something about A, but make clear that it is said for the sake of an implied statement about B. The *mashal* may make such a statement explicitly *ad hominem*: the best-known example is Nathan's "Thou art the man" to King David.[8] In this case, however, it is highly questionable whether the text should be called a fable at all, since in the first place its meaning, like that of a parable, is obscured to all but those possessing a context or key for its interpretation. In a fable whose meaning was not already transparent, this would be furnished by the concluding moral. There is a second respect in which this example from II Samuel diverges sharply from the typical fable. Nathan's reply to David, in its focused directness, undercuts the broad generality of reference that allows great specificity of application, but leaves it entirely to the whim or conscience of the reader or listener. Malicious pleasure can derive from the seemingly innocent narration of an ostensibly unrelated story about a certain vice in the presence of a person believed to be tainted by that vice; but a narrow line between fabulation and apostrophe is crossed if, like Nathan the Prophet, the narrator himself proceeds to make the obvious connection. Nathan's purpose was different from those of the tellers of fables—and it may be that the structural parallel between the Aesopic fable and the *mashal/mathal* is undercut by a divergence of intention as great as that between social satire and a theodicy or a doctrine of fate.

The fable, typically, is a story complete in itself, offering at its end an implicit, and often also explicit, "moral." But although this latter is commonly reducible to proverbial form—and proverbs, conversely, suggest the outline of an antecedent story, and should perhaps even be regarded as the condensed *moralia* of lost fables—this fact is not allowed to overshadow the story or to make it redundant. In the work of the medieval fabulists the art of storytelling, with its attention to narrative structure, rhetorical color, and characterization, and its sophisticated use of irony and wit, became increasingly important. As aesthetic considerations came into prominence, they brought the fascination of fiction that is well crafted for its own sake into a delicate and uneasy balance with the moral. With the attainment of such an equilibrium, exhibited by much of the present collection, the medieval fable stands as an achieved literary form that skillful poets could use to widen the reader's range of aesthetic and moral response.

II

The difference between eastern and western (or, as some earlier writers put it, "Oriental" or "Greek") fables can be traced in a number of ways: in the story itself, its structure, the way it is told, and in the nature of a framing story. The framing story is a characteristic of all the eastern fable-books that have come down to us, but it is not at all a feature of western fable-books. The eastern framing story generally has human personages who narrate the animal fables it contains;[9] commonly these personages are royal; their story is centered on the education of a prince, and the court intrigue that bedevils it. The Babylonian *Achiqar*, an Aramaic papyrus discovered at Elephantine,[10] is typical. Achiqar is the wise Vizier of the historical Assyrian King Esarhaddon; he seeks to rear a youth to inherit his wisdom and his title, but the boy is ungrateful, defames Achiqar, and gets him into such trouble that he narrowly excapes death.[11]

In such narratives the structure of relation between framing story and subsidiary tales is soon established, and generally maintained. Some Indian fable-books thought to derive from the *Panchatantra* have a different structure, more digressive and untidy. At a critical point one of the characters will compare the immediate situation with a fable. He will promptly be asked, "How was that?" and will proceed to relate the entire fable. In the *Hitopadeśa*, or *Book of Wholesome Counsel*,[12] which is representative of these compilations, the initial frame is effectively lost from view until the very end; as the characters of one narrative often introduce another before the completion of their own, infinite regression of the story line seems possible. Such works are digressive in another way, as well; they feature abundant moral and philosophical instruction, often extensive enough to overshadow altogether the fiction that incorporates it. This material reinforces the sense of a didactic purpose already present in the framing story—all of it belongs, directly or indirectly, to the prince's instruction—and suggests that the beast fable, if not actually allegorized by these philosophical writers, was employed by them chiefly as the vehicle of ideas.

All western fable-books but one lack a framing story, and that single exception, the general story that frames all such collections, is the history of Aesop, their legendary creator. This *Life of Aesop*, by an anonymous author,[13] explaining the origin and application of the animal fable, sets Aesop's character and story at the head of a tradition, and makes them more like a framing tale than a didactic example. Aesop first appears in Samos, where he is sold as a slave to the philosopher Xanthos, but he gains his freedom and becomes the spokesman of the people's wit and sagacity, often using his practical wit to confute the conventional wisdom of an established elite. Eventually, this role leads him into conflict with the priests at Delphi, where he is murdered, a martyr to truth and to popular wisdom. August Hausrath, contrasting this story with that of Achiqar, writes, "Compare the oriental vizier and his sententious wisdom with this figure of the superior popular sage, whose life is a struggle and whose life's breath is freedom."[14] Aesop readily became a symbol of human emancipation, and even of the rightness of the "people" in their collective judgments. If he was, as Hausrath asserts, an indigenous Greek product, this symbolic meaning of his life may have been reinforced by his emergence from a cultural matrix in which slavery was institutionalized, and whose democracy was allied to intellectual elitism.

The important motif of freedom in Aesop's biography can also be interpreted metaphorically. Aesop liberates the enchained wisdom of the folk, by making it articulate and giving it form. The content of his fables is largely familiar to his audience; the fables are homely and seem to belong to the collective wisdom of the human race.[15] Aesop broadens the social applicability of this ancient knowledge, as well as its expressive potential—and this gets him into trouble, as his differences with the Delphic hierophants suggest.[16] Aesop is a rebel against the authority of prophet and priest, as well as against the dominion of masters over slaves, and his outspokenness leads to his downfall. As a slave that is not really a slave, and a philosopher that is no traditional philosopher, Aesop is socially anomalous and ahead of his time. His story is in good part paralleled by the story of his fables. As the caustic and irreverent wit that made Aesop appealing gained an acceptable character only after his death, when he was acknowledged as the originator of something new, the new form that he invented, the fable, had to "float" for a time among existing literary and rhetorical forms before it achieved an acknowledged place and character of its own.

III

Who was Aesop? A figure partly historical and partly legendary, he is mentioned by Herodotus (*Histories* 2, 134) as having lived in the 6th century B.C. He is represented at the beginning of the *Life of Aesop* as mute. For his kindness to an itinerant priestess of Isis who has lost her way, and his devotion to the goddess herself, Isis, invoking the help of all nine Muses, rewards him with the gift of speech. With such support, Aesop could be expected to have the eloquence of an inspired poet.[17] Quick-wittedness, even before he can talk, is one of his salient characteristics. It is demonstrated when his fellow slaves gobble some figs intended for their master, and accuse Aesop of the crime. Aesop picks up a pint pot lying on the ground, and with nods and gestures requests warm water. He swallows the water, then, forcing his fingers into his mouth, vomits it up to show no trace of figs in his stomach. He then indicates that the other two slaves should undergo the same test. The contents of their stomachs proclaim their guilt, and the master exclaims, "See how one who can't even speak has revealed your deception!"

Aesop's ugliness is so spectacular as to make people seeing him for the first time ask in amazement if he is man or beast. Aesop parries this rude question with sharp repartee; the *Life of Aesop* insists that the power of reason is a more quintessentially human attribute than regularity of bodily form or feature. In his repeated demonstration of intelligence and wit, concealed by bestiality of form, Aesop resembles his own fables of beasts who present proverbial truths about the human race. In the fables, as in the *Life*, intelligence, prudence, and judiciousness in animals and human beings, are praised; stupidity, greed, and rashness are deprecated. Virtuous and vicious individuals are usually recognized, but not always judged.

Aesop brilliantly utilized fables in argument and discussion, but was apparently illiterate and did not write any of them down. The first collection of his fables in Greek prose is traditionally ascribed to Demetrius of Phalerum, a writer of the 4th century B.C. Demetrius's work is regarded as the source of the two earliest surviving collections of the fables in verse. The older of these, in Latin, is the work of Phaedrus, who wrote during the reign of Tiberius (14–37); the other, in Greek, by Babrius, is dated a century or two later. There are also prose recensions of both of these collections, as important as the poetic versions in constituting sources for medieval poets.[18] Many fables, in only slightly different versions, are common to Phaedrus and Babrius, although only Phaedrus offers anecdotes about Aesop. Phaedrus also presents many more fables about human beings,[19] and includes a number of observations about himself as poet and his standing before the critics.

A review of any comprehensive collection of Aesopic fables reveals not only a number of thematic concerns, repeated in various guises, but also some consistency in the association of particular character traits with particular creatures. For example, the physically strong and naturally rapacious carnivores—lion, eagle, hawk, wolf, and so on—are usually represented as oppressors; the weak and timid herbivores—the lamb and hare are the most typical examples—are the oppressed. Foxes and cats tend to be shifty and cunning, while dogs and asses are stolid (whether in loyalty, honesty, and virtue, or in stupidity, greed, and vainglory). Jays and crows are ridiculously vain, and sheep are silly. Goats are shrewd. All animals are shown capable of being betrayed by passion, gullibility, or pride into rebelling against their own better instincts. The typical character against which they rebel, however, is part of an established order that is stark and unyielding: the weak are weak, and the strong are strong, and the race is almost always to the swift, save where resources of character supervene.

The composers of fables were concerned with far more than bald recitation of the unchanging facts of life in a harsh world. Although it is a given that lions and hawks prey upon weaker animals, the fabulists tend to concentrate on situations intimating a possible interruption of the established pattern; they ask whether a creature acting out of character can do so sincerely or for very long—in other words, they examine the interplay between what is ascribable to nature, and what to the forces that seek or incline to modify it. These forces, typically, are the distinctively human faculties of intellect and will, broadly understood, together with such human emotions as pity and gratitude. These are the qualities by which fable transforms animals into humanoid agents, and reorders their world of simple needs and satisfactions into one of some moral complexity. The sense of reciprocity apparently governing this world, however, seems destined to repeated violation, since a major motif is that of reverting to type: the lion or eagle that adopts a pose of goodwill towards creatures usually its victims does so only because sickness or old age has affected its strength and ability to hunt; it resumes the character of predator and carnivore as soon as opportunity permits.[20] The half-frozen viper warmed in the bosom of a man no sooner recovers than it bites its benefactor (*Isopet I*, 10). Facts drawn from the natural world, in other words, do not change: it is the assumption that the human world is different, that ill-disposed and badly-intentioned humans are capable of responding well to kindness and of being changed by it, that at once tinges such animal fables with hope and edges them with a despair verging on cynicism.

Fable, then, tempers the naked violence of a dog-eat-dog world by introducing into it a variety of mediating factors, intellectual and emotional. It is suggested again and again that rhetoric and feeling incline to obscure the real nature of things. The doves or pigeons who entrust themselves to the protection of the hawk are too quick to believe its arguments, or to be convinced by their own sophistries (*Phaedrus* I, 31; *Marie de France*, 19). The sheep who make a pact with the wolves against their own guardian dogs (*Babrius* 93; also *Isopet II*, 5) are too quick to trust the enemy's glib counsel. The beasts who, overcome by their own feeling of concern, troop one by one to visit the sick lion, fail to read the evidence of the tracks that enter, but do not leave the lion's cave (*Babrius* 103). The man moved by sympathy for the snake forgets its nature. On the other hand, occasionally the predator itself is tricked, because the intended or potential victim takes the initiative in deception: for example,

Babrius 122, the fable of the lame donkey and the wolf, and even more explicitly *Isopet de Chartres* 21, the story of a horse and a lion. And in the rare case in which the typical aggressor is really well-intentioned, its genuine concern is overshadowed by the weaker creature's fear of its conventional nature: as in *Babrius* 121, the tale of the sick hen and the cat, and *Chartres* 13, of the ass and the wolf. Sometimes an unjustified expectation clouds recognition of the way things are; thus the heron's only reward for extracting a bone from the throat of a wolf is to be told that it is fortunate to have withdrawn its neck safely from a wolf's jaws (*Babrius* 94 and *Isopet II*, 1).

A readiness to be seduced by the verbal blandishments of those one ought to fear and suspect, or by an inclination to universalize one's own feelings and responses, often gives rise to self-deception. This is a considerable preoccupation of the ancient fabulists, and in itself a very fully developed theme. Its variations cover a wide range: from the case of creatures that foolishly imagine themselves to be, or to possess the powers of, differently endowed animals, to that of supposing that they continue to govern action long after it has passed beyond their control. An example of the first situation is offered by the fable of the donkey that sought to win his master's affection by emulating the antics of his dog (*Babrius* 129[21] and *Isopet II*, 4). Similarly deluded is the jay that decked itself in peacock feathers and sought to join a flock of peacocks, only to suffer repudiation by them and by its own kind, when it wanted to rejoin them[22] (*Phaedrus* I, 3; *Isopet II*, 12). Other examples are the toad who thought it could puff itself up to the size of an ox (*Babrius* 28), or the gnat who thought its weight on a bull's horn enough to disturb the bull (*Babrius* 84; in *Isopet II*, 35, a gadfly perched on a jackass). At the other pole of self-deception is the fable of the horse who enlisted the aid of a man to hunt a stag that it hated. After the hunt had ended in failure, the horse could not free itself from the rider who was now its master.[23] The fable of the frog who plotted to drown a mouse relying on it for passage across the river, only to render them both, the dead and the living, prey for the hawk, is another illustration of this idea;[24] it demonstrates that maliciousness and vengefulness recoil upon those who practice these vices.

Between these extremes of vain conceit lies a host of other instances. The familiar fable of the crow whose vanity made it lose its cheese to the fox (*Babrius* 77; *Phaedrus* I, 13; here as *Marie* 13), the stag glorying in the antlers that later trap it in the woods when its swift legs are carrying it away from the hunters (*Babrius* 43 and *Phaedrus* I, 12; *Marie* 24); the dog who considered the bell tied around its neck to warn of its treachery an ornament of honor (*Babrius* 104); the ill-favored slave girl who, because her master was infatuated with her, became a votary of Aphrodite, as if she were a beauty (*Babrius* 10); the fox convinced that the grapes it could not reach were sour (*Babrius* 19; *Phaedrus* IV, 3); the crab who thought itself of such stature as to mediate the war between the dolphins and the whales (*Babrius* 39); the mule who began to think itself a race-horse when it remembered that its mother had been a mare (*Babrius* 62), and the lizard who burst when it tried to stretch itself to the length of a snake—all these, in one way or another, express the same theme. There is also the particularly meretricious case of the wolf who, thinking itself a pious Christian and desiring to preserve its vow of lenten abstinence while at the same time satisfying its lust, decided to label the unfortunate lamb it had encountered a salmon (*Marie* 50)!

The antique fable deprecates many other forms of excess in addition to overweening ambition and conceit. One such form is greed. Everyone knows the fables of the dog who, seeking to take the reflected image of its piece of meat from the river, lost what it had (*Babrius* 79, *Phaedrus* I, 4; here as *Isopet II*, 11); and of the man who killed the hen that laid the golden eggs (*Babrius* 123).[25] The fox who eats a goatherd's leavings in the hollow of an oak finds its belly so distended that it cannot get out (*Babrius* 86);[26] and perhaps the horse whose eagerness to get into the pasture blinds it to the surrounding hedge that trips it (*Marie* 63) also exemplifies the triumph of greed over prudence.

Emotional excess, especially as vengefulness, is shown to bring misfortune or discredit upon those that yield to it: thus the fox to whose tail the vengeful farmer ties a torch bears it into his standing corn (*Babrius* 11). Pride and eminence are also sometimes singled out as the prelude to a disastrous fall. There are examples in the fables of the big and small fish in the fisherman's net, and of the fighting cocks (*Babrius* 4 and 5, respectively), as well as in those of the mice and their generals (*Babrius* 31 and *Phaedrus* IV, 6), and of the rivalry of the fir tree and the bramble (*Babrius* 64). Many fables simply poke fun at undifferentiated excess: for instance, in the tale, immortalized in the aphorism of Horace (*Ars poetica* 139), of the mountain that labors to bring forth a mouse (*Phaedrus* IV, 24; in this collection as *Isopet I*, 23). In Marie's version, a beetle crawls into the rectum of a sleeping peasant, whose agitated response to the pain gives rise to preposterous expectations of a monstrous birth among the credulous rustics, satisfied only by the insect's departure through the same opening (*Marie* 43).

The fables that express stupidity, vanity, mendacity, and lust are balanced, however, by others that exemplify the virtues of prudence, moderation, loyalty, and a sober self-knowledge that realistically accepts limitation. Of this kind are the fable of the faithful sheepdog who will not be suborned by the offer of a bribe (*Phaedrus* I, 23; here as *Marie* 20), the fables of the oak and the reeds (*Babrius* 36), and of the old and the young bulls (*Babrius* 37).

When all the varieties of human foible addressed by the Aesopic fable have been considered, one aspect, at once grim and comic, remains common to all, defining the fundamental and preponderant

form of relation in this kind of literature. It is the necessity of un-
ending search for food and for shelter from enemies and inclement
weather. The existence of the creatures of fable is characterized by
the compulsion to eat and the scramble to avoid being eaten, by the
efforts of predator and prey to outwit when they cannot outstrip or
overpower each other. This existential relation is at bottom one of
unchangeable adversaries, even when clothed in rhetoric, as of the
wolf to the lamb seeking to drink from the same stream (*Phaedrus*
I, 1; *Babrius* 89; here as *Isopet I*, 2), or given a legal form, as it is
by the dog who sues the sheep for the return of a loaf never loaned
(here as *Chartres* 11). Upon this ground, often comic, sometimes
vulgar, always quotidian, the ancient Aesopic fable traces the theme
of wisdom come too late, or wisdom attained through trial or suffering—a theme remarkably close to the *pathei mathos* of Aeschy-
lean tragedy.[27] This insight is seldom shared by the characters of the
fable, however. Classical fables deal in nothing like the high passions and terrible destinies of the heroes and heroines of classical
tragedies, but, like tragedies, they also have as their confines life
and death etched with appalling clarity. The division between tragedy and fable, in this regard, is between two treatments of these
limiting conditions of human and animal existence, between what
one might call the physics and the metaphysics of the conflict of life
and death. Fable works out this opposition in the terms noted above;
tragedy treats it in terms of honor and dishonor, the will of gods and
the will of humans, prophetic vision and the blindness of hubris.
One might then say that the ancient tragedy applies philosophical
wisdom to the metaphysical struggle for existence, and the antique
fable applies popular wisdom to the physical struggle for existence.
Poles of sensibility, as of form, their parallelism no doubt guaran-
tees that they will not meet; they may perhaps both stand as comple-
mentary expressions of the genius of a people. When we turn to the
redactions made from intermediate versions of these ancient fables

by medieval French poets, we find an altogether different literary form and aesthetic distance arising from a quite different sensibility.

IV

The medieval interest in the representation of animals over a range of styles from the naturalistic to the grotesque is reflected in the portals, capitals, corbels, and waterspouts of churches, and even in the misericords carved on the underside of the choir stalls. In literature it was expressed in the bestiary, as well as in the revival of the animal fable. I say "revival," because the classical fable tradition, as we have it, after a more or less unbroken series of Greek and Latin redactions, seems to end with the work of Avianus, who became the medieval French "Avionnet," in the fourth century. This is about the time when the first bestiaries, the *Hieroglyphics* of Horapollo and *Physiologus*, by an anonymous Syrian monk, were composed.[28] When fables began to be copied frequently again, in the tenth century, it was sometimes in the company of *Physiologus*. For example, some of the fables of Babrius are found together with this work and *Life of Aesop* in an illuminated tenth-century Greek manuscript from southern Italy, now in the Pierpont Morgan Library (MS 397).[29] Bestiaries appear to have evolved from the works of ancient natural historians, such as Pliny the Elder and Galen. Unlike fables, they followed the *Physiologus* in allegorizing the traits of animals, finding an altogether different way to make animal lore into a vehicle of truth. By the later twelfth century there was an abundance of Latin bestiaries and fable-books, fostered by the schools of naturalistic learning in such centers as Chartres and Canterbury, as well as by the large output of Latin translation from Greek, Arabic, and Hebrew sources.

The majority of these Latin Aesops are identified by the name of Romulus, an otherwise unknown figure, said to have translated the fables from Greek for his son. As might be expected, there are two basic strands to the Romulus tradition: the original prose Romulus, dated to somewhere between the beginning of the fourth century and the end of the sixth, had by the twelfth century given rise to one collection in prose, and another in verse. These are now called the Romulus of Nilant, and the Romulus of Nevelet, respectively, after the scholars that edited them in the seventeenth and eighteenth centuries.[30] The "Robert's Romulus" manuscript, so-called because in the fourteenth century it was in the library of King Robert of Naples, is another extant version of this important compilation. The Romulus of Nilant is the version of most immediate interest, however, because it was, at least indirectly, the source for the Aesop of Marie de France, who has the double distinction of being the first poetess in a European vernacular, and the first person to translate Aesop into such a language. This second claim for Marie's priority would be overthrown, however, if her own professed source were ever to be found: for she claims to have translated Aesop from an English (i.e., Anglo-Saxon) version by King Alfred the Great (871–901).

Our knowledge of Marie is disappointingly slender. Of the works generally acknowledged to be hers, the most celebrated are her Breton *Lays*, stories of love from Celtic sources.[31] She also translated into French a Latin tale of pilgrimage and spiritual renewal, *Saint Patrick's Purgatory*. Marie, although apparently of French or Flemish birth, seems to have lived and worked at the English court of the French-speaking Plantagenet kings Henry II (1154–1189) and Richard I ("the lion-hearted," 1189–1199). She names as her patron a certain Count William, and the dates of her literary activity have been deduced from attempts to identify this personage, as well as from internal evidence furnished by the manuscripts of her certain writings, and works of more dubious attribution. The arguments on this point, too technical to summarize here,[32] tell us that Marie wrote between 1160 and 1210, or even later. The *Lays* are thought to have been her earliest work, and the *Fables* came between them and *Saint Patrick's Purgatory*, probably in the last quarter of the twelfth century. The immense popularity of Marie's fables may be surmised from the fact that no fewer than twenty-three manuscript copies, all from the thirteenth and fourteenth centuries, still exist.[33]

Of the other medieval collections of French fables represented in this book, the so-called first *Isopet* of Paris (*Isopet I*) containing some sixty fables, appears to derive directly from the verse Romulus of Nevelet. Early in the thirteenth century Alexander Neckham and another Englishman named Walter produced Latin verse refashionings of the prose Romulus. Neckham's work, entitled *Novus Aesopus*, is the source for the second *Isopet* of Paris (*Isopet II*) and the *Isopet de Chartres,* both fourteenth-century adaptations in French verse. These compilations appear to have been far less widely copied than Marie's: there are only four surviving manuscripts of the *Novus Aesopus,* two of *Isopet II,* and one of the *Isopet de Chartres.* On the other hand, there remain some hundred manuscripts of the Latin verse Romulus, three of which also contain the French *Isopet I.* This work, finally, is found independently in three other manuscripts.[34]

The first and greatest of the four poets represented in this book, Marie de France, is the only one whose name we know. She used for her fables the aristocratic rhyming octosyllabic couplet that her contemporary Chrétien de Troyes employed in his chivalric romances. Marie may have chosen this metric for its appeal to the courtly milieu for which she wrote, or she may have valued the potential for satire created by the aesthetic distance between the elegance of the form and the "popularity" of her material. Marie could, when she chose, apply the lessons of her fables to feudal lords and ladies as well as to common folk. The suitability of the material to chivalric expression was much more fully exploited, however, by the anonymous poets of the following century, who produced the enormously long series of the adventures of Reynard the Fox (*le Roman de Renart*) and even earlier, in Flanders, of Ysengrim the Wolf.[35] Such treatment of the animal personages of fable remained popular well into the fourteenth century, and is reflected, for instance, in Chaucer's tale of Chaunticleer and Pertelote (the *Nun's Priest's Tale*). During the period of Marie's literary activity, however, the chivalric romance was in its first great flowering: its own long prose cycles of Lancelot and Merlin would follow only in the thirteenth century, from anonymous hands. In her prologue, Marie tells the source of her fables and emphasizes their philosophical and moral value. She implicitly compares herself to Aesop, who also composed fables for a patron. She sees the versifying of fables originally in prose as her own particular contribution to the Aesopic tradition—and it is worth noting that all of our medieval French fabulists wrote polished verse, although all but two of the received Latin sources (the Romulus of Nevelet and the *Novus Aesopus*) are in prose.

V

There are thirty-seven fables in this book. Eleven of these are by Marie de France whose collection comprises altogether one hundred and two fables, in addition to a verse prologue and epilogue.

The Fox and the Crow: Marie's version of this fable, excepting the moral, which is a feature of all her fables, falls into two parts, the first and shorter of which shows only how the crow secured its cheese. Marie subtly implicates her readers, however, with circumstantial details that go well beyond the ancient versions, and are altogether lacking in La Fontaine (see translator's note, p. 5). The pantry window, the cheeses set there, imply an unseen human whose pantry and cheeses they are: when the crow descends and snatches a cheese, the reader is ready with the thought: thief! (The adjective *thieving* is not actually in the original, but may be justified by this line of argument.) The second part of the fable is devoted to the fox's device for abstracting the crow's cheese, and begins with some play on the theme of ingenious trickery (in the French, lines 11–12: *Par engin . . . purra engignier*). Again Marie differs from both her ancient precursors and her famous follower in that the fox never addresses the crow directly. Indeed, the fox's praise for its victim's noble beauty takes the form of a prayer to God—surely an ironic echo of the old Jewish and Christian practice of blessing the Creator upon the perception of any of the beauties or grandeurs of His universe. The third-person references to the crow also make the fox's praise of it seem the more impartial, and so, perhaps, more seductive to the vainglorious bird. Perhaps the crow, "overhearing" the words of such an admirer, thinks of singing to give itself evidence in support of such marvelous praise; as Marie notes, *ja pur chanter los ne perdra* (literally, "it won't lose praise for singing"). All it has to lose is cheese. The moral is not only that the proud are inordinately eager for praise, true or false, but that they blindly dissipate their possessions in their rush to hear it. The fable incidentally contrasts a mind so enwrapped in its own delusions that it loses track of its own reality (the stolen cheese) with one perfectly attuned to real contingencies (the sudden appearance of a crow bearing a desirable cheese), and capable of engineering a deception to achieve its ends.

The Pigeons That Made the Hawk Their King: The fable uses the feudal institution of kingship to explain why any group might elect a powerful enemy as its king. The expectation is that the monarch's contractual obligations towards his subjects would overrule, or at least mitigate his characteristic violence; but the sad outcome is that the royal privilege, far from restricting bad character, is ex-

ploited by it. This seemingly cynical view is in line with a widely dif-
fused opinion in the later Middle Ages that character, not inherited
dignity, was the determinant of how kings acted. In her own moral,
Marie regards the election of the hawk by the pigeons as the bad
choice of a people free to choose otherwise, and so gives intimation
of a far more democratic political order than any actually existing
in her own age.

The Faithful Sheepdog: This fable presents the other face of
feudal obligation, and puts the vassal in a much better light than the
king in the fable just discussed. The dog holds the commonsense
view that no one gives or gets anything for nothing: its long and
eloquent defense of the mutually beneficial relation between its master and itself, like Marie's moral, asserts not only the baseness of
treachery, but the validity of the feudal order that it violates.

The Stag and His Antlers: The stag's downfall seems to be connected with the myth of Narcissus, and shows that the exclusive
contemplation of one's own beauty is as destructive when the beauty
is real as when the beauty is delusive (*The Fox and the Crow*). In
the classical sources of this fable, the stag's delight in its antlers is
accompanied by shameful disparagement of its legs; the fact that the
former imperil it while the latter are carrying it to safety sets up a
contrast between form and function and questions an aesthetic that
elevates the one above the other. Although some trace of this remains in Marie's moral, in the body of the fable she has quite suppressed it. One reason for this may have been a desire to make the
stag's contemplation of its horns as absolute as possible: like Absa-
lom, it is to be entrapped entirely by what grows from its head.
Worthy of note is Marie's play on the stag's antlers (*cornes*) and
the hunter's blowing of his horn (*cornant*), an ironic reminder that
they share the object of contemplation they view so differently.

The Peasant and the Beetle: This piece is perhaps more *fabliau*[36] than fable, not only because of the coarseness of its theme and language, but because of its human characters and its pointedly satirical rather than moral tone. The sense of intellectual elitism conveyed by the superiority of the author and her audience to the witless folk in the tale is matched by the knowing doctor's joke on the credulous rustic. In its mocking of the idea of portents, this fable is in the vein of the Horatian aphorism mentioned above and memorialized in *Isopet I*, 23; in its holding up to ridicule the suggestion that anything of significance or importance could attach to the body or feelings of such a rustic, it may perhaps offer another image of mindless solipsism like that of the crow. Marie emphasizes the gullibility of the people in the fable far more than the classical sources do, and makes a point of recording their disenchantment at the final outcome. With characteristic irony, she leaves the reader unsure whether this is due to realization that a beetle's meanderings caused all the excitement, or to disappointment that the "birth" was not more spectacular!

The Wolf's Lenten Abstinence: The wolf's mental gymnastics will have a familiar character for readers in this age of Orwellian "doublethink" and "newspeak." Its outrageous cynicism seems quite modern but, in conjunction with the fable's premise, addresses an extremely common abuse in medieval Christendom: undue lightness in the taking and keeping of vows. The Christian premise is thus allied to a Christian theme, and Marie's probable source even adds the detail that the wolf was fasting in penance for its sins. Marie seems to have turned this Christian material in quite another direction, with the wolf's internal dialogue: in structure it is a miniature of the internal dialogues of Chrétien's lovelorn knights and ladies. The moral is aimed at ungovernable gluttony and lechery. But few members of her audience would have failed to recognize in the wolf's intended victim the Lamb of God,[37] an allusion reinforced by the wolf's reference to the "costliness" of the dish. This bantering piece is the most Christian of Marie's fables, almost a parable of the ungodly man's effort to "swallow" Christ under the guise of fulfilling his precepts.

The Peasant and His Horse: The peasant illustrates a piety less seriously awry, but nonetheless misplaced. He apparently continues to understand prayer as something that can secure him a horse, even after his original horse is stolen while he is engaged in praying for a second. The imputation of the text, however, is virtually the reverse of this: to pray for a horse, when you already have one, is to assure its loss! Hence Marie's moral, whose closing word (*leialté*, "loyalty") interestingly suggests a parallel between a man's satisfaction with what God has given him and the vassal's satisfaction with the gifts of his liege. This piece, like the tale of the peasant and the beetle, is less a fable than a *fabliau* in miniature; the peasant rich enough to own a horse and greedy enough to want two may reflect the materialism typical of early bourgeois society that often figures in such stories.

The Fox and the Moon's Reflection: This fable displays not only, as the moral points out, the perils of excessive and illegitimate aspiration, but the folly and danger of reducing the unknown to the limits of one's imagination. Marie shows neatly in the middle five lines of the poem how the fox is entrapped by its own mistaken assumptions that the reflection is a cheese, and that by drinking the pond dry, it can get it. The fox's night out turns into a fatal enmeshment in its own misperceptions and foolish ambitions.

The Horse and the Pasture: This is another of Marie's many fables on the theme of desire blinding one to the obstacle in the way of its satisfaction. This fable is exceptional in its brevity and spareness. The typical introductory matter, the inward debate or conversation, the bantering tone are all absent. Marie carefully tailors her account to the substance of what it narrates: the horse sees and jumps, without reflection; her concluding moral becomes only slightly more expansive at its end with the use of two adjectives to characterize the ensuing distress (*pesanz e dure*, "heavy and harsh").

The Hawk and the Nightingale: Older versions of this fable make the hawk occupy the nest in the nightingale's absence, and demand song from it when, upon its return, it begs for the life of its nestlings. Marie has suppressed these details, and made the summons to sing come from the hawk unsolicited and unprovoked.[38] The moral that one cannot sing or speak freely in the presence of a redoubtable enemy is clear enough, though it may have a more particular area of application to the arts. While there is some irony in the portrayal of the hawk as a patron of the arts, it corresponds to a social reality: perhaps Marie meant to intimate that artists cannot do their best work if they are not free of intimidation by their patrons.

The Fox and the She-Bear: The last of Marie's fables presented here is a curious combination of fable (in its animal characters) and *fabliau* (in its blatantly sexual theme and cynical view of sexual relations). The fox's immodest proposal is described in exaggeratedly decorous form (*Forment li preia e requist / Qu'ele suffrist qu'il li fesist*, "Boldly he put the question to her, / Asking if she would let him 'do' her"), but "sets up" the she-bear, since she turns out to be an outraged prude, rather than a consenting partner. This fits these two figures into a long literary tradition in which the virtue of "stand-offish" ladies is exploited by lewd and ill-intentioned men to ruin them (some more recent examples that come readily to mind are Rabelais' Panurge and the Parisian lady who declines his suit; and the Vicomte de Valmont and Madame de Tourvel in *Les liaisons dangereuses*). The bear's fury at the fox's unchaste words is in sharp contrast with his cool admission of his character ("That's how I am"), but Marie adroitly makes her unwittingly pronounce a sexual innuendo (*Jeo te batrai od mun bastun*!, "I will beat you with my stick!") that returns to taunt her at the end when the fox answers her: "[I'm going to do] what I asked of you, [and] with which you had threatened me."[39] Like an unwelcome guest that is thrown out the door but returns through the window, the fox chased from before the bear's face returns upon its rear when, imprisoned by its own raging virtue, it cannot resist. One might expect such a fable to have a moral as simple as "Pride takes a fall" or "Overweening virtue brings about its own ruin," but Marie's seems strangely convoluted (as the translator's note suggests, p. 45). Its sense seems to be, "Clever people [represented by the fox] can get others to do what they want by words alone; they have no need of elaborate devices." But if this is so, who are those "whose wits and wisdom win the day"? They ought to be not, as appears, "some men," but the same "cunning, crafty folk." The moral seems to make the bear's downfall proceed from the fox's clever verbal taunts, rather than from its own impetuous and immoderate reaction.

Characterized by wit, irony, and psychological insight, Marie de France's fables make abundant use of dialogue and exploit it together with circumstantial detail to create dramatic effects. Drawing upon other sources in addition to the animal fable, she uses animal and human figures indifferently to exemplify her ideas. These seem to proceed from a generalized Christian ambience of thought: although the exploitation of weak by strong and the ceaseless competition for basic necessities are still present in her material, they tend to be interpreted as exemplifications of the use and abuse of mind, of the triumph of prudence or forethought over intemperance or foolishness—generally, of the capacity of the intellective powers to rule the passions. Still, she offers many examples of the reverse in ill-disposed persons. Writing within half a century of the time when rhyme first appeared in vernacular poetry,[40] she displays thorough and impressive mastery of the rhyming octosyllabic couplet, and with subtle choices of vocabulary and a wide range of poetic techniques, makes it a sophisticated instrument of dramatic dialogue as well as narrative expression. Her animal fables are a playful accommodation of the material of everyday experience and low life in high poetic form.

VI

Isopet I begins with the same famous fable that initiates Marie's work:

The Cock and the Gem: The point of this fable seems to lie in the fact that the cock, while proclaiming his indifference to the precious stone he finds while scratching in the dung, actually recognizes its worth. To reject the stone in the light of such recognition, the poet seems to be saying, is a deeper and more authentic foolishness than to remain altogether unaware of its value. Therefore, in the elaborate moral that is almost the length of the tale itself, the cock is fittingly made the symbol of folly, and the gem that of the wisdom he repudiates. In Marie's version, the cock imagines that a rich man finding the jewel would "honor" it with a fine gold setting, but he does not imagine himself as in any way constituting a "setting" for it. The concluding couplet of the moral, comparing the unstable fool to the inconstant moon, is very like the opening verse of the great Goliardic hymn to Fortune (*O Fortuna, / sicut Luna . . .*, "O Fortune, like the moon . . .*"), found in the *Carmina Burana*.

The Wolf and the Lamb: This fable comes second in *Isopet I* as in Marie's collection. The anonymous author of the fable takes care to stress, as Marie does not, the common need of drink that brings the wolf and lamb together at the same stream, although the placement of the wolf at the source (*amont*) and the lamb at the mouth (*aval*)

may suggest a hierarchical arrangement. The wolf certainly assumes
a seigneurial manner in speaking of "my drinking" and "my stream."
The fable as we have it is closer to Phaedrus than to Babrius. But in
both of the classical sources the dispute of wolf and lamb is more
extended, the lamb rebutting with simple facts each wild charge
made by the malicious wolf. The poet has concentrated instead upon
the wolf's increasing possession by the murderous impulse that has
motivated it from the start. The moral supplied is, in effect, "the
wicked always find an occasion"; another that would apply equally
well (but from the victim's point of view) is, "don't enter into argument with one that means you no good."

The Two Bitches: This is a fable of sheer ingratitude, as well as
of the foolishness of pity that goes so far as to overrule self-interest, a
theme reflected as early as line 5 in the choice of the noun to characterize the bitch that leaves its home (*la sotte*, the fool). And when
the bitch returns to claim it, it experiences the force of a proverbial
truth: possession is nine points of the law. Moreover, the suppliant,
homeless mother-to-be has become an occupying enemy with an
army. In view of all the lessons to be learned here, the poet's choice
of a moral may seem surprising: it concentrates on the treacherous-
ness of sweet words that deceive (the pregnant bitch's entreaties)
thus seeming to put a not obviously false appeal for Christian charity
on the same level as flattery, hypocrisy, and other forms of maleficent
deception. This is, in respect of its moral, the inverse of the preceding fable, making its focal point the psychology, not of the aggressor,
but of the too-trusting victim.

The Peasant and the Snake: The premise of this fable is very like
that of *The Two Bitches*: pity shown to a homeless creature almost
dead of cold. One might think, though, that the resemblance should
end with that, since the two bitches, being of the same species, share
a region of moral and intellectual discourse that does not exist here.

As suggested earlier in reference to the ancient version of this fable, the peasant has simply overlooked that it is the nature of the serpent (at least, since the fall of man) to bite and infuse poison, and should expect it to do that once it recovers its strength. It is the more interesting, then, that the poet says the revived snake "betrayed / No qualms," and supplies the little exchange between it and the peasant. His anger provokes the snake's attack upon its benefactor, and this is the point taken up in the moral, which suggests that here a natural instinct is allied with an evil disposition. In this respect the fable reinforces the common opinion often expressed in medieval bestiaries that the nature and character of animals reflects (and in some wise, results from) the moral ordering of the universe.

Reynard and the Eagle: This fable casts its two protagonists in what are in many ways their most typical roles. The fox is given the name that, as the translator explains, it bears throughout the *Roman de Renart* cycle; it is expressive of its craftiness and ingenuity. The eagle is called "king" to signify its royal prerogative of seizing whatever it desires, without regard for the rights and feelings of others. But these roles are carefully drawn into contrast with the two creatures in the character of fathers anguished by the fear of losing their children. In establishing its moral (that the strong can not only injure, but be injured by, the weak), the fable beautifully delineates the area of vulnerability both share: tenderness for their own offspring. One shouldn't forget, however, that this eagle is vulnerable on that score only because it nests in a tree, rather than, say, on a mountain top.

The Eagle, the Snail and the Crow: Another eagle fable, this one restores to the crow both the wit and the reward that so conspicuously failed it in its misadventure with the fox. Here, in fact, the credulous eagle is persuaded to let the prey it bears drop from its mouth so that the persuasive crow can seize it. In the version of

Phaedrus (II, 6), the crow and the eagle share the flesh of the victim (tortoise, rather than snail), and the moral is that none can resist the alliance of force with evil counsel. But the poet of *Isopet I* makes the crow and the eagle competitors for the snail. While the eagle is clearly the loser, the poet makes his motivation ambiguous: after the line, (literally) "he lets his prey fall to earth," he adds, "Another he can seek and pursue" (*Autre puet pourchassier et querre*), suggesting that the eagle now gives up this morsel for lost (*ceste viande a il perdue*). Its apparent indifference, together with the mention of the hunt (*pourchas*) at the beginning and end of the episode, may indicate that the eagle's real interest is the hunt, and only for a worthy prey. The moral, as so often with this poet, aims at the perniciousness of deceptive words and attacks credulity—although surely the crow has spoken truth (shown in the event) and has deceived only in the intention that the shelled snail should fall, not to the eagle, but to itself.

The Hill That Gave Birth to a Mouse: This is one of the few fables whose moral is actually longer than its main text. The text seems literally a pretext for several sententious restatements and instances of its idea that empty boasting earns not praise but well-deserved mockery. One of its interesting points is the author's allusion to his own work as *bestiaire* (bestiary: although that is a fundamentally different, if in many respects related, sort of work); another is his claim that even God mocks the braggarts, and his citation of the psalter in evidence.

The Kid That Refused Entry to the Wolf: This fable is made the vehicle for another piece of traditional wisdom: the young do well to respect and take counsel from their elders. But the body of the fable depicts with remarkable liveliness the kid's own resourcefulness: it penetrates the wolf's disguised voice, finds the peephole in the wall and looks out to confirm its suspicion, and apostrophizes the wolf so effectively that it can find nothing better than to shrink away. One wonders: did the little kid learn all that from Mother?

The Wood and the Peasant's Ax: There is some kinship between this fable and the classical fable of the pine that laments the destructive work of the ax less than that of the wedges made of its own wood, employed by the foresters to split it more easily (*Babrius* 38). The theme of giving birth to the instrument of one's own perdition is presumably the reason for the introduction of the indulgent parent and thankless child into the moral. In its lack of sympathy for the victim of aggression made possible by weapons he has himself provided, the moral seems to be denying the "turn the other cheek" philosophy of early Christians. The fable is much enlivened by the extraordinary zeal of the peasant who, ax in hand, seems to want to fell the entire wood. Opportunity transforms his latent desire into a raging obsession; this is a further thematic interest in the fable.

These examples suffice to indicate a certain loquacity of the *Isopet I* poet, especially in the morals, and a deep didactic concern that leads him to multiply instances and spare no energy to drive home his point. His verse, though polished and carefully structured, generally lacks the humor and ironic tone of Marie's, and may intimate an intended audience concerned far more with the serious import than with the satirical potential of this material.

VII

The second *Isopet de Paris* begins with a richly embellished treatment of one of the great classic animal fables.

The Wolf with a Bone Stuck in Its Throat: Babrius's version of the fable is spare enough: the wolf (apparently recognizing from the start that the heron with its long slender beak is the one best equipped to help) offers it a reward, only to send it packing after the successful "operation" with the remark previously quoted. The medieval poet opens the poem by characterizing the wolf, and situates the occurrence of its misadventure in the process of consuming an unfortunate goat. The wolf then convenes what becomes a sort of council of the beasts, offering a large but unspecified reward to whichever animal will remove the bone. Nor does the crane come forward in immediate response: after much discussion, Reynard the Fox suggests that the crane *could* do it, (literally) "if it cared to get involved" (Reynard seems to have a lively sense of the implications of doing favors for the wolf). So the wolf must repeat its appeal, this time directly to the crane, and with fresh adjurations *par sa foy* (by its faith), which the crane believes, if the fox does not. When subsequently the wolf undeceives the crane, it refers to itself as *l'aversier*—the Adversary, or Satan, and so, as in the translation, the devil—a particularly apt title, in view of its ingratitude and bad faith. The short moral goes right to the point, evoking in a single phrase (*qui cruel sert*, "who serves ruthless men") the human analogy to the world more amply delineated in the fable, where the animals circle warily about the plea of their vicious leader, trying to offset the impulse to satisfy it with a guarded acknowledgment of the dangers of doing so.

The Bat at the Battle of Birds and Beasts: In the moral the bat is called "hypocrite" (*losengier*), although it is more properly an instance of the "fence-sitter"—a type much despised in medieval opinion. Dante devised a special vestibule of hell to accommodate them, since otherwise "the damned [having taken *some* position, although a bad one] would have some glory over them" (*Inferno* III, 42). The hypocrite *does* speak from a position (which, however, he dissimulates), but the creatures represented by the bat have no position, and wait indefinitely to elect one. The bat is described as a sort of hybrid: a cat by virtue of ear and teat, but bird because of its wings, and so, at least in appearance, potentially of either of the two natures at war, though unwilling to be either the one or the other. This puts it, curiously, at one extreme of the range of hybrid beings; the opposite extreme, of course, was Jesus, partaking fully and in indissoluble union of the natures of God and man. (The generic separation of birds and beasts is taken seriously; the possibility of a species that might cross or stretch the generic boundary is not here entertained.) But that hybrid of the human and divine was unique; no creature (and in particular, no human being) can simultaneously be a thing and its opposite. In this fable an understated insistence on self-knowledge meets a thematic preoccupation with the unhappy consequences of failure to make a choice.

The Ass That Played the Hound: With this fable a poetic form different from the familiar rhyming octosyllabic couplet is introduced to this collection. In this form, much used by the *Isopet II* poet, the verses are still octosyllabic, but are grouped in sestets rhymed a a b a a b. One effect of such a metrical scheme is to break the narrative up into relatively self-contained segments, the last of which turns out to be the moral. In this fable the effects of such a structure are readily apparent: in stanza 1 the ass's lot is described; stanza 2 tells its view of the master and his dog at dinner, and stanza 3, its thoughts as to the reasons for the contrast between its life and the dog's. The next stanza, the pivotal one, describes the ass's resolve and its initial attempt to implement it. After approaching its master on its hind legs, like the dog, it seeks, in stanza 5, to embrace him, and in stanza 6, to paw his shoulder (no doubt hoping for the same gratifying effects that the dog gained from this maneuver). But in this stanza and the one following comes the ass's punishment for apparently going mad and assaulting his owner. The fable is thus quite symmetrically structured: three and a half stanzas for the rising arc of reflection, three and a half for the falling arc of action, and one for the moral. This is simple and to the point: although, as the comment above about the ancient version of this fable may indicate, it is open to other, slightly different lines of interpretation as well.

The Sheep That Betrayed Their Guardian Dogs to the Wolves: This is a complicated fable that explores the multiple meanings of loyalty and treachery. Its opening stanza announces a familiar theme: wolves are always looking for sheep to eat. But between the wolves and their intended victims stand the dogs, who vigorously and tenaciously repel the invaders—although not, it seems, with any great gusto (*Du grant mautalent qu'ils avoient*, literally "most unwilling as they were"). The reason for this seems to be that wolves and dogs are closely related species (The more likely and obvious way to read *mautalent* is as signifying merely dislike for the wolves, but the absence of *en* before *avoient*, and the ensuing verse seem to admit the possibility of the dogs' distaste for fighting with wolves, with the further implications here noted.) So the dogs, out of a sense of duty and obligation, unwillingly battle their own kind, while the wolves gratuitously plan a treacherous assault on *their* own kind, so that they can satisfy their lust unimpeded. To this end they enlist the sheep (even more self-interested than they are stupid) in a still more heinous treason,[41] inviting them to secure lasting peace from the wolves by delivering the dogs to them. The sheep, if they do perceive that the sleeping dogs are their guardians, feel abandoned by them but fail to realize that the parts in this drama remain the same, irrespective of particular enticements and particular griev-ances. The reader and author share the viewpoint of the missing shepherd, who unlike the animals themselves, fully perceives the relation of wolves, sheep and dogs. The moral—only a fool sur-renders his sole means of defense to his enemy—is a good one, but the fable is also rich in lessons about the wages of treachery, and the superiority of contractual responsibility to tribal association.

The Dog That Coveted Its Meat's Reflection: The short six-syllable lines of this fable give it the rhythm of a versified nursery rhyme.[42] It takes only two stanzas to tell the story, and the moral occupies two more: one that applies the lesson first to the dog, then generalizes it, and a second that extends the generalization with a moral law of retribution, ending with the dog as an instance of its operation. Like a number of other fables, this one contains allusions to the peril of reflections in water and implicitly to the importance of self-awareness, of knowing what one is about. What the dog covets is utterly illusory, but what it already possesses might as well be, to judge from the dog's tenuous grasp of its reality.

The Jay That Thought Itself a Peacock: The dangers of a loss of self-knowledge are explored in this fable. Its head turned by hearing itself praised, the jay turns its back upon its own kind and seeks the company of peacocks, only to suffer rejection and violence from them, and subsequently also from the jays to whom it returns. The fable is self-explanatory, expressing straightforwardly, without irony, the idea that disavowal of kin leaves one in a social wilderness, while showing how wildly a self-concept can be distorted by *outrecuidance* (overweening pride).

The Asp and the Locksmith's File: The file is an inanimate object that speaks like any of the human or animal characters of fable, a fairly common feature of the ancient fable, and to be expected where all objects and occurrences "speak" to the understanding. Here the didactic purpose seems to be powerfully present even in the premise of the fable, because it is so "denatured": the snake's instinct, no doubt, is to bite (cf. *The Peasant and the Snake, Isopet I*, 10), but its instinct would undoubtedly also guard it from the error of taking a steel rasp for food. The serpent of this fable is, from its very beginning, a figuration of the man that "bites off more than he can chew." It does seem possible, however, that the fable means to play on the hint of likeness between the long, thin, metal-colored rasp, with its ridged surface, and a snake, as if to suggest that the aggressive serpent had thought it was attacking a weaker creature of its own kind.

The Bald Peasant and the Fly: This fable presents a different form of foolish pertinacity. The fabulist has here allowed himself the pleasure of drawing the tale out to seven stanzas, emulating the repeated attacks, retreats and advances of the persistent insect and the growing frenzy of its victim. Finally, the mock heroic oath by St. Denis suggests that it is war, and comes like the solemn adjuration of a warrior sallying into battle (see translator's note, p. 117). This time the peasant has a strategy: he puts his main force behind it, and gives his maddening assailant its *coup de grâce.* In the preceding fable, the rasp on which the snake shattered its teeth was entirely passive, while here the peasant is active from the beginning, though ineffectively and to his own detriment alone, until intense irritation goads him into adding intelligence to force, and planning reprisal. But the morals of the two fables are very similar: it is, sooner (as in the case of the asp) or later (as in that of the gadfly), madness to assault an enemy more powerful than yourself. There is an added pungency in the fly's stinging the peasant about his head—the seat of his intellect, and so, ironically, the part eventually "stimulated" into deciding the insect's destruction.

"Laniste" and the Animals: This is a curious fable that seems to reduce a human character (the butcher) to animal status. In this respect it is correlative to *The Asp and the Locksmith's File*, which elevates an inanimate object to animal status. One effect so achieved is a degree of "leveling" that permits a universal discourse of things, animals, and humans. But to the extent that readers (as they were probably expected to do) keep these categories apart in their minds, quite different and deeply ironic effects are attained. For instance, in

this fable the only suggestion that "Laniste" is human comes from the similarity of his strange name to the Latin *lanius* (see translator's note, p. 121). In all other respects, he seems a beast of appalling ferocity and bloodthirstiness, far surpassing the lion, who would more commonly assume such a role in fable. In contrast, the wise but melancholy philosophizing of the bull is expressive of human sadness and resignation. The fable thus conveys, in addition to the moral adumbrated in the bull's reflections, and made explicit by the narrator, an unforgettable image of the nominally bestial as human, and of the nominally human as utterly bestial. That is at least as apt a moral for the present age as it was for the poet's.

The Gnat and the Jackass: The target of this fable is exaggerated self-importance. The issue here is not really the power to harm larger and stronger creatures, which, as another fable (*The Bald Peasant and the Fly*) has shown, the gnat certainly has; it is rather the inflated sense of one's own "weight" that the gnat of this fable exemplifies. The poet builds his ironic effect with circumstantial detail, and elaborate presentation of what is trivial ("Soon, as the sun lay sinking, / The gadfly fell to thinking"). Irony persists in the statement of the moral, where the wretched beast of burden is compared with "men of wealth and strength," and suggests the more general lesson that each perceives the world through the lens of his own concerns, and his private sense of self.

The poet of the second *Isopet de Paris*, as represented by those of his fables here translated, is a lively stylist and gives his fables an exceptionally vigorous treatment reflected in a strong story line that sometimes seems to overshadow the moral. Even where—as in *The Bat at the Battle of Birds and Beasts*—the two parts are roughly equal in length, this poet, like the other fabulists represented in this collection, leaves no doubt that a story well told can stand in its own right, and although suitably embellished by a moral, has no need of it to assert its validity.

VIII

The association of the last fable collection drawn upon for this book with the name of Chartres may bring to mind the great cathedral school that had given birth to so much distinguished poetry and natural science in the twelfth century. There is no traceable connection (nor is there any reason to expect one) between these earlier productions and the fourteenth-century compilation of forty fables here being considered; but the Latin tags preserved from the *Novus Aesopus* and appended to the *moralia* of the French versions, as well as the rather formal heading *La sentence de la fable* ("The moral of the fable") invariably employed to introduce them, may perhaps give these fables a more "clerkly" air.

The Frog, the Mouse and the Kite: The first fable from the Chartres manuscript to be included in these translations is a very famous one, found in both the prose *Babrius* and the prose *Phaedrus* and, as noted already, cited by Dante. It is a tale of treachery and malice finding their "comeuppance": the relation of the frog's perdition to its viciousness is in fact quite direct, since it is only the floating dead mouse to which the frog has tied itself that makes it visible to the kite. While both the morals castigate treachery, the Latin is more specific than the French: to betray someone that you have encouraged to trust you, or that has reason to do so, was considered particularly heinous—worse than the betrayal of one with no special cause for trust.

The Dog That Sued the Lamb: Like other fables previously noted, this one has some of the character of a *fabliau* in its preoccupation with the entanglements of the law and its cynical assertion of the way in which the unscrupulous freely offer false witness to indict the innocent. Although satire of legal proceedings and their often tenuous ties to justice is common in late antique, as well as medieval literature,[43] no specific ancient source for this fable has been identified. Here the stock character types—the evil-minded and disingenuous dog, wolf, kite and hawk against the naïve and friendless lamb—are ranged against one another in a more sophisticated version of their classic strife, the former to eat, and the latter to avoid being eaten. The venue has been shifted from the field or forest to the law-courts, the rustic setting has been "urbanized"—to such a degree that recognition of the human types in animal disguise is almost immediate. The moral reinforces such a reading of the fable: law has less to do with right and justice than with knowing how to manipulate the rules—so if you lack legal experience or counsel, forget it! The Latin moral may bring to mind the scriptural aphorism (*Matthew* xxv, 29): "Unto him that hath shall be given . . . but from him that hath not shall even what he hath be taken away."

The Lion and the Shepherd: This story is better known as "Androcles and the Lion" (see translator's note, p. 139). In general form it resembles the fable of the lion and the mouse (*Babrius* 107 and, in a somewhat different version, *Marie* 16). This fable, however, has some interesting distinctive features. Its first setting, with the wounded lion approaching a shepherd in a pasture or field, might almost be taken from chivalric romance, and the poet's use of the phrase *amours fine* to characterize the way in which the lion presents its plea enhances this suggestion.[44] The second setting is redolent of late antique Rome; the two settings together strongly suggest a medieval remaking of an ancient fable. The atmosphere of *courtoisie* is sustained throughout, vanquishing the natural adversary relationship intimated at the beginning, as well as the artificial adversary relationship created in the amphitheatre. One way in which the poet unites the two episodes is by use of the verb *connoître* (*Li pastorel conoist la chose*, "the shepherd understands the matter," v. 13 and *Bien le conoist, si court a lui*, "He knows him well, and runs to him," v. 27), implying both understanding and recognition. As the translator's note points out (p. 139), the text is rather too condensed in the crucial fourth and fifth stanzas, which have to get both shepherd and lion into the arena; but it is otherwise quite symmetrically structured, and in this respect emulates the pattern of reciprocity that is its moral.

The Sick Ass and the Wolf Physician: This fable offers a remarkably succinct comment on the power of reputation and established character. The wolf, acting out of genuine solicitude, remains nonetheless a wolf, and is viewed in the light of everything that implies. It is clear that fear of the wolf's sharp teeth makes the place that they probe the center of pain. The extended vivid image of the moral makes beautiful use of exceedingly common forms of penitence in medieval Christendom—pilgrimage *en chemise* (wearing only a shift) and fasting[45]—to suggest that a bad name is a "sin" not to be expiated, and so, graver even than murder.[46] As for the Latin tag's alteration from the form it has in the *Novus Aesopus*, one suggestion to supplement the translator's note: perhaps the poet wanted to emphasize to what a degree reputation is a matter, not of the way things really are, but of the way they *seem*, so that it suffices, for the ruin of a man's public image, that he only *appear* to be a knave. Such a deliberate emphasis would accord with this poet's profoundly skeptical view of social and political institutions.

The Horse and the Lion Physician: Here is the other side of the fable just discussed. The two fables are fairly close in the *Chartres* collection (numbers 18 and 21, respectively), but their ancient versions in the editions of Babrius are actually consecutive (121 and

122). Here the action initiated by the beast of ill repute is verbal, not physical, and the response of the putative victim is physical, not verbal. In *The Ass and the Wolf* genuine concern could not overcome fear arising from a bad name; here feigned acceptance of sham solicitude provides a space for action unmasking and frustrating the evil designs of the predator. Interestingly, the lion indicts itself for troubling to play the doctor when it enjoyed superior force that alone would have sufficed to secure its ends: naked aggression would have served the lion better! And the poet seems to think the latter a nobler, or at least, more honest path of action for the lion, since the moral asserts that one resorting to low tricks that are beneath him will be brought down by just such vile devices. The lion, then, is not seen here as predator alone; there seems to be an accompanying sense of the lion as king of beasts and so, unworthy of the fraudulent ploy by which it seeks to ensnare the horse.

The Horse That Wished to Hunt the Stag: This fable not only illustrates how lust for vengeance brings down the vengeful; it is a parable of the loss of freedom, and, as previously noted, is quoted as such by Aristotle. Indeed, it might well have been used illustratively by political theorists of all ages, such as Thucydides, Machiavelli, and Montesquieu. The horse is shown to be totally under the sway of its hatred, and the fabulist makes it clear that in the grip of such strong emotion it is at a distinct disadvantage to the hunter upon whom it calls for assistance, and who is not slow to realize the opportunity thus afforded him. Initially, the stag is the quarry of both horse and hunter, but as the object of the hunt recedes into the background, the new relation between the hunter and his mount is increasingly asserted. One can imagine the horse's subjection as the outcome even if the stag had been taken; the horse's unperceived "bird in the hand"—its freedom—turns out to be worth more than

any number of hunts, successful or not, with its new and too powerful ally.

The Ant and the Cricket: The translator has chosen to end his
selection with the fable that begins La Fontaine's. This Old French
version of the famous fable emphasizes the industriousness of the
ant, making it a sort of paragon of the bourgeois virtue on the rise
throughout Europe in the fourteenth century. Perhaps the phrase
Ce n'est pas mauves vaselage is intended, not altogether without
irony, to stress the distinction of the ant's self-reliance, foresight, and
inexhaustible self-serving energy from the less conspicuous virtues
of the obsolete feudal order. But if the ant is a paragon of virtue, it
is certainly not Christian virtue: the charity that would dictate the
sharing of one's bread with the hungry (even if totally "undeserv-
ing") is wholly lacking here. This fable may accordingly recall the
"dog-eat-dog" world of the ancient fable, where the struggle for existence is unrelievedly just that. But there is a further dimension to
this fable that may make it a particularly apt one to terminate this
collection. The cricket failed to gather and store food because it had
another occupation: it was a singer—in other words, an artist. The
fabulist thus brings to mind—as did Marie and others, in their versions of this fable—that amid the playfulness of art, and the preoccupation of its practitioners with its refinement and perfection,
they cannot afford to neglect the earning of a livelihood. Patronage—particularly as here, after the fact—is a slender hope, at best.[47]
Marie's version, not included in this book, hints at this difficulty, in
the cricket's account of itself to the ant: *"Jeo chantai," fet il, "e
deduis / a altres bestes, mes ne truis / ki me vueille guereduner."*
("I sang," said he, "and entertained / Other beasts, but find no one /
that is willing to reward me").

Parting from the Chartres poet and his three predecessors is accordingly on a note that soberly brings back down to earth poets and readers that have indulged themselves in the exuberance of song and the sophistication of technique. The moral and conclud-ing Latin couplet of this fable unequivocally support the ant's se-verity, but leave room to wonder how accurately they reflect the poet's feelings. The fable seems to express far more than the smug confidence of the ant, and to leave its readers in doubt as to whether there would really be room for poets—and Christians—in a world dominated by the ant's views: even for poets able, like this one, to satirize their own calling and the precariousness of their economic status.

IX

Fables seem to have been transmitted from place to place and from people to people for as long as they have existed. The lore of fable itself incorporates many stories such as that of the Persian vizier Achiqar, summoned to teach his wisdom to the king of Egypt. And since the communication of fables has led to their being writ-ten down, it has had a further consequence in the unceasing trans-lation of fables: from popular to learned languages, as the Hitopa-deśa from Prakrit to Sanskrit; from eastern languages to western languages—and vice versa; from one classical language to another; and again, in both east and west, from classical languages to medie-val and modern vernaculars. The history of the translation of fable would be very nearly as long and complex as the history of fable itself. The translations now offered to the reader, however, belong to a tiny segment of this vast history of translation, and so absolve us from immediate concern with most of it. I shall try here to deal briefly only with "modern" English translations of Aesop (taking Caxton's work printed in 1484 as a convenient starting point), and shall give particular attention to verse translations.

Caxton's translation, like the great majority of Aesop translations made since his time, is in prose. An obvious reason for the
translation of poetry into prose is that it is far easier to convey
"meaning" straightforwardly when one does not have to worry simultaneously about meter, rhyme, and so on. The counter-argu-
ments to this view are just as evident: poetry comprises more than
what its words seem to say, its "content" is indissolubly wedded to
its form; but translators of Aesopic fables, especially if they worked
in a time and place favorable to the opinion that the value of these
fables resided predominantly in their *moralia*, might have found
such arguments for verse translation weak and unconvincing, against
the virtues of clear expository prose. Of course, there are many other
good reasons for making verse translations: the literary aspirations
of the translator, his sense of the literary value of the fables, the need
to be faithful to the originals (also an argument for prose if one
considers "fidelity" differently), the greater challenge posed by
verse, and no doubt, the sheer enjoyment of it. In general, as some
of the examples quoted below will illustrate, verse translators have
been far more free with the Aesopic material than have their counterparts writing prose, often moving it decisively in the direction of
parody and satire.[18] And almost all previous English verse translations that identify their sources derive from Latin or Greek originals
rather than, as here, the Old French.

Many English prose translations of Aesop, like Caxton's, begin
with a statement of the moral, and go on to present the fable as an
illustration or exposition of it. This is not only to overemphasize the
exemplary character of the fables, but runs contrary to the medieval
French practice, and to that of most of the classical and medieval
Latin antecedents. It is particularly to be noted in editions of the
later seventeenth and eighteenth centuries. More recently, even prose
translations have been restored to their position of superiority over
the morals, and several twentieth-century editions have suppressed

the morals altogether. The most notable of these is that of L. W. Daly, who advertises this feature in his title: *Aesop Without Morals*. But the morals were certainly important to Caxton, to Thomas Myddleton, whose translation was published in 1550, and to the Elizabethans, who also cherished Golding's "moralized" Ovid (1567). At the close of the following century (1694) came the prose translation of Sir Roger l'Estrange, which has been one of the most celebrated and reprinted prose versions of Aesop.

One of the most impressive of post-Elizabethan verse translations of Aesop is that of John Ogilby, printed in a handsome volume adorned with many fine woodcuts ("sculptures") at London in 1651. Ogilby keeps his morals short, or at least they seem so in contrast with the texts of the fables, somewhat ponderously embellished and elaborated to many times the length of the originals. For instance, in the fable of *The Horse and the Lion Physician* (*Chartres* 21), he gives the lion fully forty lines of debate about whether to take up Law, Divinity, or Medicine. The manner in which the lion argues its way to rejection of the first two and election of the third may remind the reader of nothing so much as the entry upon stage of Marlowe's Faustus.

An anonymous translation of 1655 gives its source as the Greek. Its ironical *Epistle to the Reader*, signed " X Y Z &c," calls the animal characters of its fables ". . . Metaphoricall Nick-names for Rationall Creatures possest with such Qualityes and Dispositions. . . . in brief, the whole story of late times represented as in a Mask by these irrational Actours." This volume, adorned with some 235 woodcuts, offers each of its fables in both a prose and a verse version! The prose renderings are generally accurate; perhaps on that account, the verse takes considerable license, adding or deleting entire episodes. As a sample I quote this poet's version of *The Fox and the Crow*:

The Crow had got a prey, and with it flies
To feed upon a Tree: which *Vulpes* eyes,
And fain would gull her of it; wherefore he
To work his plot, thus greets her craftily;
Hail, Mistrisse, hail, Fames untruths now I sing,
And to your worship joyfull tidings bring.
Fame stiles thee black as Soot, but I have found
Her rumours false, in whitenesse you abound
Beyond the snow, or lillies of the field.
For which the joyfull Crow seems thanks to yield,
Clapping her wings. But as she strove to speak,
The bait she had dropt from her empty beak.
    Which the fox nimbly catching, leaves the Crow
    To learn more wit when she is flatter'd so.

Another anonymous translation, printed at Cambridge in 1697, offers verse of a rather more popular character, with many feminine rhymes; its version of *Reynard and the Eagle* gives a fair sample.

An Eagle that thought a young Fox pretty victual,
Wou'd carry some home to her birds that were little:
The Old Mother Fox ran after protesting,
And from her claws mercy most humbly requesting;
When all other arguments failed, and were slighted,
She fetches a firebrand that was well lighted:
Saies she, for my sake no pity is shown,
Yet now Mrs Eagle, show some for your own:
For if you return not my Cubs at desire,
I'le set both the tree and your nest in a fire:
The Eagle was startled at this proposition,
And gave back the cubs with an humble submission.

MORAL

The Powerful ne'er should their Greatness abuse,
Inferior Persons to vex or abuse:
No Creature so dull its designs to pursue,
But rage makes 'em witty and mischievous too.

Eighteenth-century poets (excepting such as the mischievously satirical ones whose output is mentioned in note 48) were less reticent about their names. The earnest and sententious Edmund Arnaker, Rector of Donaghmore (Ireland) and Chaplain to the Duke of Ormond, published in 1708 his Aesop with lengthy "improving" Morals padded by apposite (and not so apposite) cullings from the Scriptures. In some cases he also appended suitable quotations from classical authors. Here, without the added citations of Juvenal and Claudian, is his rendering of *The Pigeons That Made the Hawk Their King*:

The Doves and Kite:
Or,
A rash Choice, repented

The Doves wag'd War with their old Foe, the Kite,
And chose a Hawk to Head them in the Fight:
He undertook it, but abus'd his Pow'r,
And strove, not to protect them, but devour.
The Helpless Birds, to greater Harms betray'd,
Dearly repent the fatal Choice they made;
And rather wou'd the Kite's insults sustain,
Than their new Tyrant's sanguinary Reign.

MORAL

Few Men in any Station acquiesce,
But shift, and change, tho' still without Redress:

So rarely Heav'n a lasting Blessing finds
To gratifie our inconsistent Minds:
Manna, tho' suited to each wanton Gust,
Cou'd not long silence Isra'l's murm'ring Lust:
They Egypt's Bondage, more than Freedom, priz'd;
For Leeks and Onions, Angels Food despis'd.
This fickle Humour is a wild Disease,
Whose raging Fits no Med'cine can appease:
Nor is it strange we thus Inconstant prove,
Who, with Discretion, neither Hate, nor Love.

On the other hand, Bernard de Mandeville, author of *The Fable of the Bees*, who published some verse translations of Aesop under the title *Aesop Dress'd* in 1704, writes with a more worldly tone (reflected, in the following quotation, in his mention of "Interest" and "Principal"—although that allusion is present in La Fontaine's version, a few decades earlier). As his translation of *The Grasshopper and Ant* shows, Mandeville was sensitive to its implications for "a Musician or a Poet," and suggests that only such a one would really be in a position to understand the grasshopper's plight.

The Grasshopper and Ant

A Merry Grasshopper, that sung
And tun'd it all the Summer long,
Fed on small flies, and had no Reason
To have sad thoughts, the gentler Season:
For when 't was hot, the Wind at South,
The Victuals flew into his Mouth:
But when the Winters cold came on,
He found he was as much undone,
As any insect under Heav'n;
And now the hungry Songster's driv'n
To such a state, no Man can know it,

But a Musician or a Poet.
He makes a visit to an Ant,
Desires he would relieve his want;
I come not in a begging way,
Says he, No Sir, name but a day
In July next, and I'll repay
Your Interest and your Principal
Shall both be ready at a call.
The thrifty Ant says truly Neighbour,
I get my living by hard labour;
But you, that in this Storm came hither,
What have you done when 'twas fair Weather?
I've sung, replies the Grasshopper;
Sung! says the Ant, your Servant, Sir;
If you have sung away the best
Of all the Year, go dance the rest.

A last example from the eighteenth century, however, is from a poet that chose to remain anonymous, and indeed did not have his publisher date the work, although he assures his readers that one of its distinctive features is the provision of "new morals." His *Mountain in Labour* reads as follows:

A Mountain was swell'd to so monstrous a Size,
That some wonderful Thing was expected to rise,
And burst ope the Womb of the Labouring Earth,
Which seem'd to contend, and to struggle for Birth;
And what shou'd become of this vast Preparation,
But there creeps out a Mouse?—Which Baulked all
    Expectation.

MORAL

Great Promises must not from all be believ'd;
There are few who give Credit but find they're deceiv'd.

Nineteenth- and twentieth-century verse translations of Aesop are less numerous than one might suppose. One Victorian wag, who signs his pamphlet only "P. J.," translated several dozen fables with remarkable concision into limericks, followed by one-line morals. Here are three of them that will be recognized as having their counterparts in the present collection:

> A Snake took to gnawing a File:
> He was hungry. He gnaw'd it a while
>   To no purpose. The Steel
>   Only thought—I don't feel
> Your sharp teeth: you can't chew up a File.

We may meet our match.

> The Horse ask'd the Man for his aid,
> 'Gainst the Stag, of his great horns afraid.
>   Man help'd: all the worse
>   For the fool of a Horse
> The slave of his rider was made.

You may pay too much for success.

> The Wolf wanted Lamb for his dinner.
> Said he, "You once wrong'd me, you sinner!
>   If it was not quite you,
>   'Twas your grandmother Ewe:
> So you must be had for my dinner."

Evil will can always find an excuse.

The novelist Oliver Herford published a collection of fifty versified fables in 1921. All are couched in regular iambic tetrameter couplets; none have separate morals. This is an example of his style:

The Gnat and the Bullock

A Gnat, once chancing to alight,
After a long and weary flight,
Upon a Bullock's horn to rest,
With a loud buzzing thus addressed
The Bullock, "Pray, good Sir, allow
Me to express my thanks; and now
If you don't mind, I'll fly away,
Unless you'd rather have me stay."
"Pray do whatever you decide;
'Tis all the same to me," replied
The Bullock; "I was not aware,
Until you spoke, that you were there."

These examples, various as they are, may help to show some of
the originality of the present translations, viewed simply as instances
of English verse. It is not the present purpose, nor is it within the
scope of this introductory essay, to offer literary analysis of these
translations. The preceding remarks, meant to supplement the translator's notes, are based predominantly on the French originals. The
translations themselves, in respect of their colloquial vivacity and
vigor, fidelity to the content, prosody, and tone of the originals, and
extraordinary energy are unique. Some of their other conspicuous
virtues—such as exceptional skill in the achievement of unforced
rhymes, ingeniousness in word choice and application, the seeming ease of alliterative and onomatopeic effects—while impressive,
can find parallels in the work of one or another predecessor. It should
be remembered further, however, that these are in all probability
the first English verse translations to be made of these Old French
fables: the translations quoted above stem (where sources are di-
vulged) from Latin or Greek originals. The translations in this book,
accordingly, do not merely extend, revise, or refurbish an older,

standing body of English verse translation: rather, they originate, bring to life in English, a new body of poetry corresponding to an older tradition that has until now been accessible only to those who read various dialects of a medieval language. Under these circumstances, the energy of these translations may be expected to differ, as in fact it does, from that of the originals; but it succeeds in imparting to them a freshness that it is hard to believe they did not possess for their first readers and auditors.

A good translation succeeds in bringing past and present together in its own union of innovation and conservatism, allying its meticulous effort to preserve the style, thought, images, and feeling of the original with its daring attempt to find a modern equivalent for the radical newness of the original in its own day. There is a distinctive aptness in the present translator's enterprise, since he puts into twentieth-century English twelfth-century French poetry whose authoress claimed to have translated it from an even older English book. The evidence that such literary vicissitude exists, joining the culture of one particular time, place, and language to that of another by its own extraordinary and unpredictable alchemy, offers heartening reassurance of at least a thread of continuity in human experience; and the vitality and versatility of the wisdom that Aesop taught assert the existence of another thread, complexly and inextricably intertwined with the first. This is the endurance of art, and of its infinite capacity to transform thought and experience. What is ultimately to be learned from Aesop's fables, beyond their particular morals, is how mutually self-informing and self-enriching art and experience are; and that the fruit of their interplay is not only instruction and enlightenment—but pleasure.

—HOWARD NEEDLER

Middletown, Connecticut

MARIE DE FRANCE

THE FOX AND THE CROW

I ssi avint e bien puet estre
Que par devant une fenestre,
Ki en une despense fu,
Vola uns cors, si a veü
Furmages ki dedenz esteient
E sur une cleie giseient.
Un en a pris, od tut s'en va.
Uns gupiz vint, si l'encuntra.
Del furmage ot grant desirier
Qu'il en peüst sa part mangier;
Par engin voldra essaier
Se le corp purra engignier.
"A, Deus sire!" fet li gupiz,
"Tant par est cist oisels gentiz!
El munde nen a tel oisel!
Unc de mes ueiz ne vi si bel!
Fust tels sis chanz cum est sis cors,
Il valdreit mielz que nuls fins ors."
Li cors s'oï si bien loër

Qu'en tut le munde n'ot sun per.
Purpensez s'est qu'il chantera:
Ja pur chanter los ne perdra.
Le bec ovri, si comença:
Li furmages li eschapa,
A la terre l'estut chaïr,
E li gupiz le vet saisir.
Puis n'ot il cure de sun chant,
Que del furmage ot sun talant.

C'est essamples des orguillus
Ki de grant pris sunt desirus:
Par losengier e par mentir
Les puet hum bien a gre servir;
Le lur despendent folement
Pur false losenge de gent.

They tell the tale—quite likely
    true—
About a thieving crow, who flew
Close by a pantry window, spying
Cheeses inside set out for drying.[1]
Needless to say, the prospect pleased
Our feathered friend, who swooped
    and seized
One of them in his beak, escaping.
Promptly a fox appeared, and—
    gaping—
Ogled the cheese with lustful eyes,
Thinking how he would gormandize
That luscious morsel, if the crow,
Properly hoaxed, would let it go.
And so, he feigned great awe: "God
    love me!
Look at that beauteous bird above me!
Never before have eyes beheld
Such loveliness unparalleled.
Ah, could his voice but match his
    features,
Then would this fairest-formed of
    creatures
Truly surpass all worldly treasure!"
The crow, puffed up with pride and
    pleasure
(So had the fox's praises moved him),
Thought that, indeed, it well
    behooved him
Now to display his songbird side.
"Awk awk!" he croaked, beak open
    wide.

Out fell the cheese... It hit the
    ground...
The fox was there—one leap, one
    bound—
Pouncing, purloining, nibbling,
    gnawing,
Deaf to the crow's confounded
    cawing.

This goes to prove how preening
    folk—

1. A comparison with the opening lines of
La Fontaine's version of this fable, perhaps his
best known ("Maître Corbeau, sur un arbre
perché, / Tenait en son bec un fromage . . ."),
gives good example of some of the subtle
divergences that can exist between different
adaptations of the same basic material.
Nowhere does the seventeenth-century poet
tell us how his crow came by the famous cheese.
(Marie, on the other hand, will not bother to
specify where her crow is perching.) Though
such differences are often traceable to the
immediate models of each adaptor, at other
times they are the fruit of the individual's
artistic preference, whim, or even the need to
make a rhyme. La Fontaine's probable model,
Phaedrus, was specific enough: "Quum de
fenestra Corvus raptum caseum / Comesse
vellet celsa residens arbore . . ." (I, 14). Marie's
model is lost and we cannot be sure what
liberties she has taken. (For that matter, Aesop's
crow wasn't carrying a cheese at all, but a
chunk of meat!)

Pompous and overweening folk—
Fall prey to blandishment and bluff.
Sweet, wheedling words are quite
    enough:
Lie to your heart's content. No matter!
More will they give, the more you
    flatter!

THE PIGEONS THAT MADE
THE HAWK THEIR KING

Colum demanderent seignur.
A rei choisirent un ostur,
Pur ceo que meins mal lur fesist
E vers altres les guarantist.
Mes quant il ot la seignurie
E tuit furent en sa baillie,
N'i ot un sul ki l'aprismast,
Qu'il n'ocesist e devorast.
Pur ceo parla uns des coluns,
Si apela ses cumpaignuns.
"Grant folie," fet il, "fesimes,
Quant nus l'ostur a rei choisimes,
Ki nus ocit de jur en jur.
Mielz nus venist que senz seignur
Fussuns tut tens qu'aveir cestui.

Einz nus guardiüm nus de lui,
Ne dutiüm fors sun aguait;
Puis que nus l'eümes atrait,
A il tut fet apertement
Ceo qu'il fist einz celeement."

Cest essample dit a plusurs,
Ki choisissent les mals seignurs.
De grant folie s'entremet,
Ki en subjectiün se met
A cruël hume e a felun:
Ja n'en avra se hunte nun.

The pigeons—so the story goes—
Longed for a king. At length they chose
The hawk, the theory being that he
Would rout their every enemy
And let them live in peace. But oh,
How far awry some theories go!
Whenever a pigeon came within
The new king's grasp, he did him in,
Gobbled him up, and gulped him down.
Dissent soon rose against the Crown:
"What fools were we," one bird bewailed
Before the flock, "when we prevailed
Upon the hawk to be our ruler.
Daily his deadly deeds grow crueller.

Better to have no king at all!
Before he came, we could forestall
His distant threats to life and limb,
But then we went and sent for him!
Now he can do, without restraint,
What once he did by fraud and feint."

This exemplary tale is meant
To chide those churls whose lives are spent
As willing slaves to scurvy lords:
Such knaves will earn their just rewards.
Those who a ruthless rascal serve
Reap the disgrace they well deserve!

THE FAITHFUL SHEEPDOG

D'un larrun cunte ki ala
Berbiz embler, qu'il espia
Dedenz la falde a un vilein.
Ensemble od lui porta un pein;
Al chien voleit le pain baillier,
Ki la falde deveit guaitier.
Li chiens li dist: "Amis, pur quei
Prendreie jeo cest pain de tei?
Jeo nel te puis guereduner:
Fai a tun ués le pain guarder!"
Li lere dist: "Jeo n'en quier rien.
Manjue le pein, sil retien!"
Li chiens respunt: "N'en vueil niënt!
Jeo sai tresbien a esciënt
Que ma buche vuels estuper
Que jeo ne puisse mot suner,
Si emblereies noz berbiz;
Kar li bergiers est endormiz.
Traï avreie mun seignur,
Ki m'a nurri desqu'a cest jur;

Malement avreit enpleié
Qu'il m'a nurri e afaitié,
Se par ma guarde aveit perdu
Ceo dunt il m'a lung tens peü.
E tu meïsmes m'en harreies
E pur traïtur me tendreies.
Ne vueil tun pain si guaaignier."
Dunc comença a abaier.

Par essample nus mustre ci:
Chescuns frans huem face altresi!
Se nuls li vuelt doner luier
Ne par pramesse losengier
Que sun seignur deie traïr,
Nel vueille mie cunsentir;
Atendre en deit tel gueredun,
Cume li chiens fist del larrun.

About a thief the tale is told,
Who spied some sheep within a fold,
And thought it might be passing
   pleasant
Forthwith to filch them from the
   peasant
Whose beasts they were. "Look here,"
   he said,
Tempting the watchdog, "have some
   bread...
Present from me to you..." However,
Sensing deceit in his endeavor,
Deftly the dog declined his offer:
"Empty of purse and bare of coffer,
How can I buy your bread?"
   "Pooh-pooh,"
Countered the thief, "you
   misconstrue.
You needn't pay me. Here, it's free."
"Nonsense," replied the dog. "I see
Clearly enough what you're about!
You'll stuff my mouth so I won't
   shout
And wake my master, fast asleep,
While you make off with all his sheep.

What? Would you have me thus
   betray
The shepherd who, unto this day
Has fed and sheltered me? How could
Such evil now repay such good?
Indeed, in conscience, how can I
Undo the wealth he feeds me by?
Even the likes of you, I warrant,
Would find such faithlessness
   abhorrent!
No, you can keep your bread!" So
   saying,
He filled the air with bark and baying.

Thus should all honest men and true
Do as our dog was quick to do.
When smooth-tongued knave with
   bribes untoward
Would pay them to betray their lord,
Let them remain unmoved, aloof,
Scornful of gain and flatter-proof.
Then, like the thief in this, our tale,
His foul design is doomed to fail.

THE STAG AND HIS ANTLERS

Issi avint qu'uns cers beveit
A une ewe, kar sei aveit.
Guarda dedenz, ses cornes vit.
A sei meïsmes a dunc dit
Que nule beste nel valeit
Ne si beles cornes n'aveit.
Tant entendi a sei loër
E a ses cornes esguarder,
Que il vit venir chiens curant
E lur mestre, ki vient cornant;
Aprés lui vienent, sil quereient,
Pur ceo que prendre le voleient.

El bois se met tuz esmaiez.
Par ses cornes est atachiez,
En un buissun est retenuz.
Dunc sunt li chien a lui venuz.
Quant il les vit si aprismier,
Si se cumence a desraisnier.
"Veirs est," fet il, "que li huem dit
E par essample e par respit:
Li plusur vuelent ceo loër
Qu'il devreient suvent blasmer,
E iço laissent qu'il devreient
Forment loër, se il saveient."

A thirsty deer was standing by
A stream and drinking, when his
    eye—
Suddenly, as he sipped—was caught
By his reflection. "Ah!" he thought,
"What handsome, shapely horns
    have I!
No hornless beast, I vow, can vie
With likes of me..." And on and on
He sang his praise; until, anon,
He spied a pack of hunting hounds,
Spurred by the huntsman, heard the
    sounds
His horn blared forth, as they drew
    near
With one intent—to bag the deer.

Trembling, he turned to flee, and
    started
Into the wood... He dashed, he darted,
He flew... But all at once, betwixt
Branches and boughs, he stood
    transfixed:
A tree had caught his horns!... The
    pack
Grew closer now, would soon attack...
"Alas, alack!" he sighed, distraught,
"How true it is, as man has taught,
That we, too often, blindly prize
Those things that we had best despise;
While in our folly we abhor
Those we should well be thankful
    for."

THE PEASANT AND THE BEETLE

JK

D'un vilein dit ki se giseit
Cuntre soleil, si se dormeit.
A denz s'ert mis tuz descoverz,
E sis pertus esteit overz.
Uns escharboz dedenz entra,
E li vileins s'en esveilla.
Grant mal li fist, tant qu'a un mire
L'esteit alez cunter e dire.
Li mires dist qu'il esteit preinz.
Or fu mult pis qu'il ne fu einz;
Kar li vileins bien le creï,
E li fols pueples, ki l'oï,
Diënt que c'est signefiance.
En poür sunt e en dutance;
N'i a celui ki bien ne creie
Que granz mals avenir lur deie.

Tant est li fols pueples muables,
Qu'en veines choses nunverables
Unt lur creance e lur espeir.
Le vilein guaitent pur saveir
Par unt cil enfes deveit nestre.
Li escharboz par la fenestre,
U il entra, s'en est eissuz:
Dunc furent il tuz deceüz.

Par cest essample le vus di:
Des nunsachanz est altresi,
Ki creient ceo qu'estre ne puet,
U vanitez les trait e muet.

A loutish lummox lay a-dozing,
Flat on his face, his arse exposing
Unto the sun, with cheeks spread
    wide;
When lo! a beetle crawled inside
The grandly gaping aperture.
Needless to say, the brutish boor
Awoke at once, in pain, and hied him
Straight to the doctor, who, to chide
    him,
Told him he must be great with child.
Stupider than before, he smiled
In daft belief, then went to tell
All of his friends, who, daft as well,
Saw in the news a portent grave.
Looking with awe upon the knave,
They sat in wait for Fate to strike.
For that's what fatuous folk are like:

Easily swayed, their minds are not
Immune to trash and tommyrot.
They thrive on foolish folderol.
And so they waited, one and all,
To see just how the babe would
    come...
At length the beetle, venturesome,
Appearing—much to their chagrin—
Came out the same way he went in.

This moral fable teaches us
That witless folk were ever thus:
Though tall the tale, they're quick to
    swallow—
Where folly leads, there will they
    follow!

the wolf's lenten abstinence

JK

Jadis avint qu'uns lous pramist
Que char ne mangereit, ceo dist,
Les quarante jurs de quaresme;
A tant en aveit mis sun esme.
En un bois trova un multun
Cras e refait, senz la tuisun.
A sei meïsme demanda:
"Qu'est ceo," fet il, "que jeo vei la?
C'est uns multuns, ceo m'est a vis!
Se pur ceo nun que j'ai pramis
Que nule char ne mangereie,
De sun costé me refereie.
Ore ai," fet il, "parlé folie!
Jeol vei tut sul senz cumpaignie;
Ceo m'est a vis, se jeo nel guart,
Tels i vendra d'alcune part,

Ki l'en merra ensemble od sei,
Si nel larra nïent pur mei.
Jeo puis bien prendre le multun,
Sil mangerai pur un salmun;
Mielz valt li salmuns a mangier,
E sil puet l'um vendre plus chier."

Si vet d'ume de malvais quer:
Il ne puet lessier a nul fuer
Sun surfet ne sa glutunie;
Ja encuntre sa lecherie
Ne huem ne femme lecheresse
Ne guardera vou ne pramesse.

A wolf announced his firm intent
To spend the forty days of Lent
Fasting from meat of every kind.
He little knew that he would find
A fat young lamb, while wandering
    through
The wood! Alas, what could he do?
He asked himself: "What's that I
    see?
Looks like a lovely lamb to me!...
Oh damn! Without that silly vow,
I could be eating lamb chops now!
Why did I have to swear that I
Would eat no meat? Oh my, oh my!
Here I am, all alone with this
Soft, luscious lamb! How can I miss
So fine a chance? If I don't grab him

Somebody else is sure to nab him,
Whisk him away... And I won't get
Even a blessèd bone, I bet!
No, no! I'll take the lamb, and merely
Call it a salmon, loud and clearly.
Salmon's a fine and costly dish...
And I can eat my fill of fish!"

Creatures of evil temperament,
Try though they may, cannot prevent
Their gluttonous lust from holding
    sway:
How many oaths and vows will they
Blissfully break, to take their leisure
Hot in pursuit of fleshly pleasure!

the peasant and his horse

JK

D'un vilein cunte ki entra
En un mustier e si ura.
Un suen cheval aveit mult chier,
Si l'atacha hors del mustier.
A deu requist qu'il li aidast
Qu'un altel cheval li donast.
Tant cum il fist ceste ureisun,
Sun cheval emblent li larrun.
Quant il fu del mustier eissuz,
Si esteit sis chevals perduz.
Ariere vet hastivement,
Si prie deu devotement

Qu'altre chose ne requereit
N'altre cheval mar li durreit,
Mes face li aveir le suen,
Kar il n'avra ja mes si buen.

Pur ceo ne deit nuls huem preier
De plus aveir qu'il n'a mestier:
Ceo guart que deus li a doné,
Si li suffise en leialté!

A certain peasant—so they tell
    us—
Rode up to church and, duly zealous,
Wanted to pray. But first he tied
His true and trusty steed outside.
Once at his pew, our pious peasant
Begged that the Lord make him a
    present:
Another horse as fine and fair.
While he was thus engaged in prayer,
Thieves came, alas, and stole his horse.
The peasant—much distressed, of
    course,
When he came out to find it gone—

Turned on his heel and, thereupon,
Ran back to pray that God ignore
The prayer he'd uttered just before:
"Forget that second horse!" he cried.
"Bring back the first—my joy, my
    pride!"

God frowns on those whose greed is
    such
That they, too often, ask too much.
So don't complain about your lot:
Be glad to have what good you've got.

THE FOX AND THE MOON'S REFLECTION

JK

D'un gupil dit ki une nuit
Esteit alez en sun deduit.
Sur une mare trespassa.
Quant dedenz l'ewe reguarda,
L'umbre de la lune a veü;
Mes ne sot mie que ceo fu.
Puis a pensé en sun curage
Qu'il ot veü un grant furmage.
L'ewe comença a laper;
Tresbien quida en sun penser,
Se l'ewe en la mare fust mendre,
Que le furmage peüst prendre.
Tant a beü que il creva:
Iluec chaï, puis n'en leva.

Meinz huem espeire, ultre le dreit
E ultre ceo qu'il ne devreit,
Aveir tutes ses volentez,
Dunt puis est morz e afolez.

A fox, they say, his leisure
taking—
Out for the evening, merry-making—
Started to cross a pond; when lo!
He saw the moon's reflection—
though
He had no notion, actually,
What such a curious thing could be.
After a bit of introspection,
It struck the fox that said reflection
Must be a cheese. And so, he hung
His head down low, and with his
tongue
Began to lap the water, thinking—
While thus he gulped and saw it
sinking—

That soon the cheese was his... But
first,
He drank, drank, drank... and
promptly burst.

How many the men whose aims are
such
That they aspire to far too much!
Reaching for goals unwisely
cherished,
Many have suffered, many have
perished.

the hawk and the nightingale

Ci nus recunte d'un ostur,
Ki sur le fust s'asist un jur,
U li russignols ot sun ni
E u ses oiselez nurri.
A sei le prist a apeler,
Si li cumanda a chanter.
"Sire," fet il, "jo ne purreie,
Tant cum si pres de mei vus veie.
Se vus plaiseit a remuër
E sur un altre fust voler,

Jeo chantereie mult plus bel;
Ceo sevent tuit cil altre oisel."

Altresi vet de meinte gent:
Ne pueent pas seürement,
La u il dutent, bien parler,
Si cum la u n'estuet duter.

A hawk out for his daily flight,
Looking about where he might light,
Lit on a tree—so goes the tale—
That housed a mother nightingale
And all her brood. No sooner landing,
Gruffly he summoned her, commanding
Her to come near and sing her song.
"Good sir," was her reply, "as long
As you're so close, I must say, sadly,
I cannot sing. But I'll sing gladly—

Far better too, my friends agree—
If you go find some other tree!"

As with the nightingale, so too
With many a human creature who,
Though eloquent and glib of tongue,
When faced with fear comes all
     unstrung.

the horse and the pasture

JK

Uns chevals vit u herbe crut
Dedenz un pre, mes n'aparçut
La haie dunt fu clos li prez:
Al saillir enz s'est astelez.

Ceo funt plusur, bien le savez:
Tant coveitent lur volentez,
Ne veient pas quel aventure
En vient aprés pesanz e dure.

A horse espied, by meadow's edge,
A patch of grass, but not the hedge
That kept him out. He went to jump,
Leapt for the mark... and broke his
   rump.

Many's the headstrong man whose
   whim
Has almost been the death of him.
He brooks no doubt, no hesitating,
Blind to the woes that may be
   waiting.

THE FOX AND THE SHE-BEAR

JK

D'un gupil nus recunte e dit,
Ki une urse trova e vit.
Forment li preia e requist
Qu'ele suffrist qu'il li fesist.
"Tais," fet ele, "malvais gupiz,
Ki tant par iés chaitis e viz!"
"Jeo sui," fet il, "tels cum jeo sueil,
Sil te ferai estre tun vueil."
"Fui," fet ele, "laisse m'ester!
Se jeo t'en oi ja mes parler,
Tenir te purras pur bricun:
Jeo te batrai od mun bastun!"
Tant l'a li gupiz enchalciee,
Que l'urse s'est mult curuciee.
Aprés curut pur lui ferir,
E il fuï, pur li traïr,
Tant qu'il la meine en un buissun.
Les espines tut envirun
L'unt atachiee e encumbree
E par la pel l'unt detiree,

Si qu'el ne pot avant aler
Pur nule rien ne returner.
Dunc revint li gupiz ariere;
Sur li sailli par de deriere.
L'urse cumença a criër;
Puis si li prist a demander:
"Malvais gupiz, que feras tu?"
E li gupiz a respundu:
"Ceo que jeo t'oi," fet il, "preié,
Dunt tu m'aveies manacié."

Ceo deit ester e remaneir,
Que pruzdume dira pur veir:
As veziëz est bien a vis,
Que lur parole est en tel pris
Cum li engins de meinte gent,
Ki par cunseil venquent suvent.

A fox approached a she-bear, bent
On lewd and lecherous merriment.
Boldly he put the question to her,
Asking if she would let him "do" her.
"Shut up!" she shrieked, in highest
    dudgeon.
"Foul, filthy fox! Cur, cad,
    curmudgeon!"
The fox replied: "That's how I am!
But let me tell you something,
    Ma'am:
Don't be so proud, or you'll regret it.
Like it or not, my pet, you'll get it!"
"Leave me alone, you lout!" she
    shouted;
"More stupid talk and you'll get
    clouted!"
Dauntless the fox pressed on, until
The angry bear had heard her fill.
She turned to box his ears... He ran...
She followed... And the chase began.
The wily fox dashed off apace,
Straight for a thickly wooded place,
Bristling with bushes, barbed and
    prickly.
Boldly the bear plunged in... Too
    quickly!
Brambles and thistles pricked her
    skin:

The thicket held her, hemmed her in.
Gloating, the fox strode up beside her,
Promptly proceeded to bestride her,
Pressed his advantage from behind...
The bear howled, growled, groaned,
    wailed and whined,
And asked the fox just what he
    wanted.
"Come, come, my dear!" the victor
    taunted.
"You were so proud, you silly sot,
    you!
I said I'd get you... Well, I've got
    you!"

And so, as every wise man knows,
Most cunning, crafty folk suppose
Their tongues alone possess the skill
To bend their victims to their will—
Tongues, like those snares that some
    men lay
With wile and wit, to win the day.[2]

2. Several other possible morals spring to mind
for this fable. Marie's is, I think, rather
unexpected. But it is the one she wrote, and I
have resisted the temptation to alter it
significantly.

isopet i

the cock and the gem

Un coc en un fumier estoit;
Du bec bechoit, des piés gratoit,
Comme pour sa viande querre,
Tant que une precieuse pierre
Et mout riche a trouvé ou fiens.
Cil a cui il n'en fu a riens
Dit con cilz qui riens ne la prise:
"Riche pierre, mal ies assise,
A moi ne pues tu faire preu;
Trop es herbegiee en ort lieu.
Se li trouvierres qui deüst,
Si com je t'ai trouvé t'eüst,
Mieux fust ta grant biauté vehue
Et ta grant bonté cogneüe.
Tu ne m'affiers, ne je a toi;
Je ne te vuil, ne tu vues moy."

LA MORALITÉ

Iceste pierre senefie
Sagesce, et le coch la folie.
Sens et folie, se me samble,
Ne s'acordent pas bien ensamble.

L'en dit que le nombre infenit
Sus les fos point ne se fenit.
Le fol demoustre sa folie
Partout la ou vet en oÿe.
La condicion des gens saiges
Tourjours amende leurs coraiges.
Le fol se mue com la lune;
N'est en li fermetés aucune.

50

A cock upon a dunghill perching,
Scratching with claw and bill, was
    searching
Something to dine on in the dung;
When all at once he found, among
The morsels of manure, a rare
And precious stone. With scornful air
Of one who prized it not a whit,
He said: "Rare jewel, why must you
    sit
There in the muck! It's plain to see
You're of no earthly use to me!
If you had been discovered by
Someone more fit for you than I,
Then you would see your beauty
    prized
And your perfection recognized.
You don't need me, and—*entre
    nous*—
I have as little use for you."

THE MORAL

This stone denotes intelligence;
The cock betokens lack of sense.
Wisdom and folly—I doubt whether
They can go hand in hand together.

He who counts fools, they say, will be
Still counting, come eternity.
Let them but speak: no sooner heard,
Fools will be fools with every word.
In wisdom does the wise man find
Enrichment for his heart and mind.
The fool is like the moon, however:
Constantly changing, constant never.

THE WOLF AND THE LAMB

Un loup et un aigniau enmainne
Soif, pour boire a une fontainne:
Le loup amont, l'aigniau aval.
Cis qui ne panse fors a mal
Rudement a dit a l'aigniau:
"Pourquoy me troubles tu mon eau
Et nuis a boire, di le moi."
Cils qui a peeur et esmoi
Dit que il n'y a de riens neü,
Combien que ait du russel beü:
Ne puet yaue monter arriere,
N'oncques pour ce n'an fu mains
     clere.
"Comment, me manaces tu
     doncques?"
Dit l'aigniau: "Sire, non fis oncques."
"Si feis," dit le loup, "par saint Pere!
Tout autel fist jadis ton pere:

Pour li morras, a li retrais!"
Cils qui ne quiert fors bien et pais
N'i puet trouver pais ne acorde
Que le desloial ne le morde:
Morir le couvient sens raison.

LA MORALITÉ

Tout aussin fait le mauvais hom:
Achoison sen cause pourchace
Comment au preudomme mesface.

Qui vuet faire division
De ami, tost quiert occasion:
Met sus a son ami la raige,
Si con nous tesmoigne le saige.

A wolf had stopped beside a
brook.
About to drink, he chanced to look
Downstream, and saw, exposed to
view,
A lamb whom thirst had brought
there too.
The wolf, whose every thought and
action
Turned in a trice to malefaction,
Thundered: "How dare you spoil my
drinking
And foul my stream!" The poor lamb,
shrinking,
Quaking with fear and weak of knee,
Said that he failed to see how he
Could foul the stream—unless, of
course,
The water flowed from mouth to
source.
"So!" growled the wolf, "you think
you're clever,
Lecturing me!" "Oh no, Sire, never!",
Answered the lamb. The wolf, eyes
wide,
Swore by the Holy Father, and cried:
"Oh yes you do, I vow! What's more,
you
Do as your father did before you!
Die, then, for him whom you
resemble!"

Helpless, the meek, mild lamb,
atremble,
Died in the wolf's unyielding jaws.

THE MORAL

The wicked need no proper cause
To do their ill: the least excuse
To harm the just will suit their use.

One need but forge a vain pretense
To do one's fellow foul offense.
Your dog's a nuisance? Claim he's
mad:
Though false the charge, the beast's
been had![3]

3. My translation strays from the text only
enough to clarify its intent. The original alludes
to an Old French proverb, "Qui bon chien veut
tuer, la raige li met seure," meaning, literally,
that anyone who wants an excuse to destroy
his dog need only claim that he is rabid. Or,
as Randle Cotgrave's celebrated *Dictionarie
of the French and English Tongues* (London,
1611) explains it: "When a bad Prince would
be rid of a good subiect, or seruant, the tricke
is, to lay treason to his charge." By Cotgrave's
time the proverb was already well established.
It has been traced at least as far back as the
13th century. (See Antoine Le Roux de Lincy,
Le Livre des proverbes français, 2 vols.
[Paris, 1842], 1:109.) The same proverb, in
modern dress, has persisted to the present: "Qui
veut noyer son chien l'accuse de la rage."

the two bitches

Une chiene povre et truande
Prie a une autrë et demande
Que pour Dieu li prest son hosté,
Tant que si flanc et si costé
De ses chaiaux fussent delivre;
Et la sotte l'ostel li livre,
Si s'en va ailleurs pourchassier:
Bon loisir a d'aller chassier.
Tant a venu, tant a alé
Que l'autre lisse a chaellé.
A son lieu vient et si demande
Que celle son ostel li rende.
Celle li fait la sourde oreille
Et ferme bien l'uis et veroille;
Et celle dehors la menace,
Pour ce cuide que issir l'en face;
Mais d'illuec ne l'en puet chassier
Par prier ne par manessier.
L'une de doleur se courrouce,

Et l'autre s'enhardie et grouce,
Qui se sent avecques ses chiens.
L'autre voit que ne li vaut riens
Et qu'elle est seule, si s'en vet;
Bien voit qu'elle a perdu son plet.

LA MORALITÉ

Qui croit paroles doucereuses
Souvent les treuve venimeuses.

Le dous chant deçoit l'oiseillon;
L'enfançonnet, le papeillon.
Quant plus doucement la serainne
Chante, a li les nageurs amainne:
Aucune fois les faut morir
Quant l'en ne les puet secourir.

A poor and pregnant bitch approached
A bitch more fortunate, and broached
A grave request: she prayed the other
(Seeing her soon to be a mother)
Kindly, for love of God, permit her
Use of her house to have her litter.
Foolishly she agreed, at which
The soon-to-be-delivered bitch
Blithely moved in as she moved out.
The benefactress went about
Her business—hunting game, and
    such—
Until the birth. Then, inasmuch
As her good deed was done, she went
Back to her house, with clear intent.
Bitch number one snarled: "Not a
    chance!",
Turned a deaf ear and looked askance,
Shutting the door with lock and chain.
Threats, pleas, persuasion—all in
    vain:
She would not budge. The row grew
    hotter.

"I have my children," growled the
    squatter.
"See? You're outnumbered!" Which
    was true.
All by herself, what could she do?...
Bitch number two, to her dismay,
Knew she had lost, and skulked away.

THE MORAL

He who would swallow words too
    sweet
May well get poisoned ones to eat.

The fledgling bird is lured by song;
The butterfly flits blithely along
Into the youngster's grasp; and when
The siren sings, how many the men
Who row to meet her, faster and
    faster,
Steering their course for sure disaster!

THE PEASANT AND THE SNAKE

En yver, quant gelee prent,
Un vilain trouva un serpent
De froidure ainsi comme morte.
Li vilains la prent si l'emporte
Pour le aisier, en son osté,
Com cil qui en ot grant pité.
Si l'aisa au mieux que il pot,
Et celle grant mestier en ot.
Dou froit la gardë et dou vent;
Mès l'en rent mal pour bien, souvent.
Quant le serpent fu en bon point,
De mal faire ne se faint point:
Son venin gita ça et la.
Adont le vilain l'apela:
"Issiés," dit il, "fors de ceans!"
Mès de l'issir est il neans;

Vers li se trait et si le mort
Tant que son hoste a laissié mort.

LA MORALITÉ

Ainsi rendent li mauvès tuit
Mal pour bien et painne pour fruit.

Une souris qu'est en escharpe,
Le bien dedens menjue et harpe;
Et le feu qui est au giron
Art et destruit tout environ.
Le serpent qu'est en sain cachiés
Fait au seigneur mout de meschiefs.

One winter's day a peasant found,
Lying upon the frosty ground,
A frozen snake—not dead, but
    dying—
In need of quick revivifying.
Pitying such a hapless plight,
The peasant mused on how he might
Rescue the snake. And so, he took
The creature home, found him a nook
Safe from the wind and wintry air,
And tended him with loving care.
But good is often ill repaid:
Restored to health, the beast betrayed
No qualms, but presently dispensed
His poison round about. Insensed,
The peasant cried: "Be off! Begone!
Out of my house!..." But thereupon

The snake, attacking him instead,
Bit him and left him quite, quite dead.

THE MORAL

Thus do the treacherous folk disburse
Evil for good; for better, worse.

Safe in your sack, a mouse will gnaw
    on
Everything he can put his paw on.
So too the passion-fire within you
Burns you to bits—flesh, bone and
    sinew.
He in whose breast a viper lurks,
Soon learns what harm his venom
    works.

REYNARD AND THE EAGLE

L'aigle, qui est roy des oisiaus,
Embla un de ses renardiaus
A Renart, pour ses aigliaus pestre.
Renart, qui dolent en dut estre,
Mout li pria, mout li requist
Que son renardiau li rendist.
Oncques l'aigle ne li vost rendre.
Renart pot oïr et entendre
Que son fils près de mort estoit
Se consoil en li ne metoit;
Et bien vit que force n'avoit
Ne pooir; s'engin ne savoit,
Comment se vengast dou meffet?
Sous l'aubre ou l'aigle ot son ni fet,
Buche vert et chaume assambla,
Si ne sai ge se il l'embla.
Mout y sot bien le feu bouter;
La fumee prist a monter
Jusque aus aigliaus qui ou ni furent:
A bien petit que mort ne furent.
Li aigles voit que ses aigliaus
Estaignent, soit li lait ou biaus.

Sa proie li couvient laissier,
Autrement ne s'en puet passer.

LA MORALITÉ

Par cest flaviau poués entendre
Que li grans puet bien nuire au
        mendre
Et li mendres puet nuire au grant,
Si comme avés oÿ devant.

A la fois li victoriens
Au vaincu rechiet es liens,
Et le petit, par son engin,
Abat le grant de son engin.
Aucune fois cils puet bien nuire
Qui a aidier ne se puet duire.
Bien puet po, qui ne puet blecier;
Tel nuit, qui ne puet adrecier.

Monarch of all the birds, the
    eagle—
Wishing to feed his eaglets regal—
Pounced on the fox and snatched away
One of his young. "Ah, welladay!",
Bewailed Reynard,[4] "alas, alack!",
And begged that the babe be given
    back.
Cold and unmoved, the eagle spurned
His pleas: the tot was not returned.
At length Reynard, distraught,
    discovered
How close to death his offspring
    hovered.
He knew that all was lost unless
He used his fox's artfulness,
His one and only weapon now
Against the mightier foe... But
    how?...
And so, to venge the deed, he laid—
Under the tree where the eagle made
His nest—a pile of twigs and thatch
(Most likely filched!), fired up the
    batch,
And stirred it till the tree stood
    smoking.
The eagle gaped: his chicks lay
    choking—
The pretty ones, the ugly too—
Gasping their last... What could he
    do?...

In short, paternal anguish pricked
    him:
To save his brood, he freed his victim.

THE MORAL

This fable proves to us that, though
The strong can always wreak their
    woe
Upon the weak, the weak are able—
As you have heard—to turn the table!

The victor oftentimes will fall
Into his victim's snare; the small,
Thanks to their artful feints, at length,
Topple the great, despite their
    strength.
Though some may seem too meek to
    dare
Indict a mighty foe, beware!
Many's the way to right a wrong:
Strength is not only in the strong!

4. In calling the fox by his proper name, instead
of by the generic term *goupil*, the Old French
poet gives evidence of the broad popularity
of the *Roman de Renart*, the 12th- and 13th-
century collection of animal stories in which
the shrewd trickster plays a central role. The
name, inherited from widespread Germanic
tales, means "strong in counsel." (For an
exhaustive study and extensive bibliographical
reference, see John Flinn, *Le Roman de Renart
dans la littérature française et dans les
littératures étrangères du moyen âge*
[Toronto, 1963].)

THE EAGLE, THE SNAIL
AND THE CROW

Li aigles ala en pourchas;
Ce jour ne prist fors un limas.
Li limas crient que cil li nuise:
Tost se boute dedens sa cruise.
A l'aigle dit lors la cornile:
"Ce que vous en ceste coquile
Portés, ne vous vault une poire;
Mès se vous me voliés croire,
Il vous vaudroit aucune chose,
Qu'il a dedens viande enclose;
Mès la coquille la vous tost:
Brisiés la, si charra tantost.
Engin couvient a la brisier;
Bien le vous savrai devisier:
Lessés la a terre cheoir,
Apertement pourrés veoir
Que sus les pierres brisera;
Ja elle si fort ne sera
Pour quoi elle chee de haut."
Li aigles, qui croire la vaut,

Lesse cheoir sa proie a terre;
Autre puet pourchassier et querre.
Ceste viande a il perdue;
La cornille s'en est peüe.

LA MORALITÉ

Male langue par sa parole
Tout le monde engine et afole.

L'en ne doit mie tantost croire
Que chascune chose soit voire,
Car par trop grant credulité
Chiet l'en en grant necessité.
Oÿ dire va par la vile;
Qui trestout croist, forment s'avile.
A celi doit l'en imputer
Qui creance fait abuter.

The eagle, off to hunt his prey,
Had spent a rather fruitless day:
One lowly snail was all he'd caught.
The latter feared the worst, and
    sought
The safety of his shell, withdrawing.
At length the crow appeared and,
    cawing,
Flew up abreast. The winged intriguer
Eagerly eyed the eagle's meagre,
Niggardly loot. "Avast," he cried,
"There's lots of tender meat inside
That pretty little shell. Except,
Of course, it's worthless if it's kept
Hidden away... How can you take it?
Simple! You drop the shell and
    break it.
Easy as that, the meat falls out.
You understand? Just fly about
Until you spy some rocks below—
Good solid ones—then let it go.
The shell will give, I guarantee!"
The eagle acquiesced. Thought he:
"Clearly the crow's advice is sound."

And so he circled round and round...
Stopped... Dropped the snail... It hit...
    It burst...
Down swooped the crow and got
    there first!

THE MORAL

What woe the wicked tongue can
    wreak:
To work its wiles, it need but speak.

Beware lest you accept as true
Tales that are blithely told to you.
Some simple souls—naïve,
    believing—
Leave themselves ripe for cruel
    deceiving.
Others there are who, like the rabble,
Gladly give ear to buzz and babble.
Better for them if they rejected
Villainous prattle thus confected.

the hiLL that gave birth
to a mouse

A une place qui plainne yere,
Enfla la terre en tel maniere
Que il y ot un si grant mont
Que trestuit grant peeur en ont
Cils du païs communement,
Et cuident bien certainnement
A ce que l'enfleüre montre
Soit senefiance de montre.
Tel paour ont toutes et tuit
A pou que chacuns ne s'en fuit;
Mès il ont peeur sans raison
Car, quant ce vint en la saison,
Oncques n'issi fors que souris:
Or est passés tous li perils.

LA MORALITÉ

Aucuns mout hautement menacent
Et puis si quierent qui le facent.
Maintes gens a pou d'achoison
Ont grant peeur en leur maison.

Les montaignes a grant planté
Une souris ont enfanté.
Le saige de l'anflé se moque
Quant ce qu'il dit tout vient a gogue.
Mieux vaut pou parler et plus faire,
Ce trouvons en ce bestiaire.
Qui de vamter c'est atourné,
Moqueeur a tantost trouvé.
Personne par sa vanterie
Ne sera pour ce plus prisie;
Nostres sires les moquera:
Ou psautier ce trouvé sera.

74

A certain patch of level land
Began one day to swell, expand,
Rise from the ground, protruding,
    bulging...
Fearful, the simple folk, indulging
Forthwith their rustic superstition,
Thought that this most untoward
    condition
Augured, indeed, the imminent birth
Of some fierce monster spawned of
    earth.
So frightened were they, one and all,
At what misfortunes might befall,
That most began to flee, until
Straightway the danger passed. The
    hill
Presently came to term: it bore
A mouse!... A mouse, and nothing
    more!

THE MORAL

Some who will thunder threats
    portentous
Tell us, anon, they never meant us;
Thus is there many a soul who, truly,
Fusses and fears and frets unduly.

Pregnant, the hills grow fat; and yet,
Mice will be all their pains beget.
So with the braggart proudly puffing:
The wise man knows he's only
    bluffing.
Many a fable, tale, opuscle
Preaches this rule: "Less tongue, more
    muscle."
Actions, not words—that's what
    we're after!
Nothing but scornful, scoffing
    laughter
Follow the brash and boastful sort.
Even Our Lord himself makes sport:
Witness His hymnal, wherein ample
Lessons abound, to good example.

the kid that refused entry to the wolf

La chievre va querre viande
Pour son chevrel et li commande
Et amonneste que du toit
Ne se mueve, ou il estoit:
Car, s'il s'en part, saiche de voir
Il y puet bien dommaige avoir
Tel dont il se tendra pour fos.
En l'ostel l'a laissié enclos.
Si comme il fu demourés sous,
Este vous Ysangrin li Loups
Vient a l'uis et boute et apelle
Et change sa vois et chevrelle:
"Euvre l'uis," dit il, "a ta mere!"
"Non feré," dit il, "par saint Pere!
Assés y pourrés appeler:
Bien vous connois au chevreller,
Tant le sachiés vous contrefaire;
N'enterrés ja en mon repaire.
Et si voi bien par un pertuis
Que j'é ci trouvé en cest huis
Que vous estes uns loups de voir

Qui me voulés ci decevoir;
Ailleurs vous estuet querre proie."
Ainssi le chevrel l'en envoie.

LA MORALITÉ

Pour ce vous di qu'a l'enfant vient
Grant preu quant il voit et retient
La bonne doctrine du pere;
Et qui nou fait, il le compere.

Les ensaingnemens ne trespasce
Des grans, ne ne met en espasce
De pere et mere la doctrine:
En ton cuer les garder ne fine.
En ceci croi les anciens
Se vuis estre victoriens.
Con les anciens croist jonesce,
Mauvitiés en cuer ne les blesce.

A she-goat leaves her hungry kid
Snug, safe and sound at home, amid
Instructions, orders, threats galore
To stay inside and lock the door
While she goes off to find some
    dinner.
If not, the silly little sinner
Will come to grief. And so, we find
    her
Carefully shutting the door behind
    her.
Time passes by. And then: a visit!
There, large as life... Good gracious,
    is it?...
Yes, Isengrim the Wolf,[5] by name,
Wily of wit and foul of fame!...
Knock knock! "Who's there?" "It's
    me." " 'Me' who?"
Counterfeiting a bleat or two,
The wolf replies: "Why, pet, it's
    mother.
Come, let me in." "Tell me another!",
Answers the kid. "By God, you'll
    never
Set foot in here! Oh yes, you're
    clever,
Changing your voice that way, and all.
But there's a hole here in this wall,
And I can peek and see you're lying:
Friend, you're a wolf, there's no
    denying!
Go pick some simpler prey to
    plunder!"

Off slinks the wolf, hopes dashed
    asunder.

THE MORAL

So goes an axiom elemental:
Son who accepts wise words parental
Reaps a reward both good and proper.
He who rejects them comes a cropper.

Don't be the child who disrespects
Adult advice, or who neglects
His parents' teachings; rather
    endeavor
To keep them in your heart forever.
You youngsters who would taste
    success,
Don't trust your callow youthfulness.
Listen to age. Its strength will arm
    you:
Trouble may strike, but will not harm
    you.

5. Isengrim—whose Germanic name ("iron mask") presents many variant spellings in Old French—figures in several episodes of the *Roman de Renart*, as the fox's antagonist and dupe. He was originally the hero of a medieval Latin satirical poem of his own, the lengthy *Ysengrimus* by Nivard of Ghent, composed around 1150 (and edited, in more recent times, by Ernst Voigt [Halle, 1884]). The name, however, seems to have been attributed to the wolf at least several decades earlier.

THE WOOD AND THE PEASANT'S AXE

Une coignie ou faut un manche,
Dont nuls ne cope ne ne tranche,
Ot en sa maison uns vilains.
Au bois pria q'un de ses rains
Li donnast pour un manche avoir;
Et li bois, par son nonsavoir,
Li octria legierement,
Dont se repentira briefment.
Enmanchié a cils la coignie
Puis l'a a deus poins empoingnie:
Le bois commença a abatre.
Non mie deus ne trois ne quatre,
Mès du meilleur et du plus bel
Abat et met en un moncel.
Le bois, qui s'est donné la mort,
Dit que sa folie l'a mort:
"De ce qu'au vilain ai baillié
Suis," dit-il, "roupt et detaillié."

LA MORALITÉ

Nuls homs son anemi ne doit
Garnir de chose, quel que soit,
Dont perils li puisse venir,
S'il ne se vuet pour fol tenir.

Qui armes baille a anemi,
S'il muert, estre ne doit gemi.
Qui le sien trop largement donne,
Pourra ouïr encor ramponne.
De ce maillet ou de plus gros
Puisse avoir cils rompus les os.
Qui donne tant a son enfant
Que puis il va son pain querant,
Puis après a dongier menjue,
Ferus soit de ceste maçue.

A peasant owned an ax; that is,
Part of an ax—the blade—was his.
But blade alone, with handle lacking,
Won't do much hewing, chopping,
    hacking...
And so he went and asked the wood
For just one branch, from which he
    could
Fashion a proper shaft, attach it
Fast to his blade, and make a hatchet.
Quickly the innocent wood
    consented—
And then, more quickly still,
    repented!...
The peasant takes his new-made ax,
Goes to the wood, and promptly
    hacks
Tree after tree—not two, three, four,
But all of the best—trees, trees
    galore!
Now, from the depths of melancholy,
The dying wood laments his folly:
"Into his grasp, alas, I placed
The murderous arms that lay me
    waste!"

THE MORAL

Only the man on madness bent
Will put the ruinous instrument
Of his destruction, darkly planned,
Into his enemy's eager hand.

Let no one mourn the man who dies
By arms that he himself supplies.
Rather let such a generous fool
Be mauled and clubbed with ridicule:
That best of bludgeons, hammered
    to him,
Promptly will shatter, dash, undo
    him.
So too, the father—gulled,
    beguiled—
Who heaps his all on thankless child:
When he himself must beg his board,
Scorn's cudgel-blows are apt reward!

isopet ii de paris

the wolf with a bone stuck in his throat

Uns leus qui fu de male part,
Glout et enfrun et de mal art,
S'enossa, par mesaventure,
De l'os d'une chievre qu'iert dure.
Quant enossé fu, si requist
Les bestes sauvages et dist
Que qui l'os oster li porra,
Grant guerredon li en fera.
Les bestes parlerent ensamble:
"Par foy," dist Renart, "il me samble
Que la grue bien le guerroit,
Se entremettre s'en voloit."
Le leu la commence a prier
Que elle se hast de lui aidier,
Et quan qu'elle demandera,
Par sa foy, il li paiera.
La grue si crut sa parolle:

Sa teste et son col, comme folle,
En la geule au leu a lancie;
Hors en trait l'os, si s'est drecie
Et dist au leu que il li doit
Grant louier et que il li pait.
Dist li leus: "Mont te dois prisier
Quant de la geule a l'aversier
T'es issue sans mal avoir:
Autre louier n'en pues avoir."

Qui cruel sert, si doit aprendre
Qe guerredon n'en doit atendre,
Mais douter se doit de domage
Et garder s'en, se il est sage.

A wily wolf—ill-born, malicious,
Gluttonous, glum, and avaricious—
Having himself a meal of goat,
Suddenly stopped: down in his throat
A bit of bone sat firmly stuck.
(A hard one, too!) Cursing his luck,
He called his fellow beasts, and
    pledged
A rich reward if one unwedged
The blasted bone and freed his gullet.
They heard his offer, paused to mull it,
Argued the matter round about,
Until, at length, Reynard cried out:
"I do declare! There's one who
    could...
The crane can do it, if she would!"
And so the wolf besought the bird,
Promising, with his solemn word,
To give her—if her skill relieved
    him—
All she desired. The crane believed
    him.

Into his mouth she plunged her bill—
Long neck and all—and pecked until
The bone had been retrieved. But
    when
She stood before the wolf again,
Asking for her reward, he said:
"You should be glad you have your
    head,
Snatched from the devil's jaws!
    I've let
You keep your life. That's all you'll
    get!"

You who serve ruthless men must
    learn
Never to look for rich return.
Take care, instead, to mind your skin:
Be wise, beware... or be done in!

the bat at the battle of birds and beasts

Bataille fu d'oisiaus volans
Encontre les bestes courans,
Grande et mortel et perilleuse
Et de chascune part douteuse.
L'aleur fu plaine de boisdie,
De barat et de tricherie.
Il s'apensa que il faindroit
A chascun que des siens seroit,
Et quant ensamble chapleront,
A ceus se tendra qui vaintront.
Aus oreilles et a la teste
Sembloit mieus chat que autre beste;
Aus eles oysel resambloit:
Raison ert, car oisel estoit.
Sa fauseté si fu seüe
Et des. .II. pars aperceüe:
Chascuns le het et le deffie,
Nuls ne fu au las en aïe.

Le losengier, si com moi samble,
Quant il voit ses voisins ensamble
Troublez, faint, par losengerie,
A chascun qu'est de sa partie;
En l'oreille va l'un blaumant,
A l'autre refait autretant;
La haïne fait confermer
Que il fait semblant d'afiner.
Quant sa fauseté est seüe
Et des .II. pars aperceüe,
Chascuns le het, n'en doutés mie,
Et refuse sa compaignie.
Comme l'aleur est demenez,
Qui d'estrange et de privez
Fu haï par sa tricherie.
Mal ait cil qui vit de tel vie!

The beasts of land and birds of air
Were locked in battle. Everywhere
War dealt its death and dole about,
While victory long remained in
  doubt.
The bat, creature of dark deceit
And cunning craft, thought it was
  meet
That he profess his loyalty
At once to both sides equally,
Intent—when broil and brawl were
  done—
To rally round the winning one.
(In shape of ear and teat,[6] the bat
Was not, in fact, unlike the cat;
Yet, with his wings, he seemed to be
A bird—and bird indeed was he.)
In time, his treason stood revealed
To both sides of the battlefield;
And by both was he thereupon
Disdained, despised, left woebegone.[7]

The hypocrite, should he perceive
Two friends at odds, will make
  believe
He sides with each. With vile pretense
He courts both parties' confidence:
Feigning to quell their enmity,

To each he whispers calumny
Against the other, till, at last,
Their hate is hardened, firm and fast.
But once his treacherous deeds are
  known,
He reaps the ills his fraud has sown!
For both combattants then despise
  him,
Turn on the wretch and ostracize him.
Thus is the traitor then undone,
Just like the bat, whom everyone
Condemned for his duplicity.
Woe be to such a one as he!

6. The original *teste* is a variant spelling of *tette*, and should not be confused with the Old French word for "head." The Latin original of the *Novus Æsopus* cites the bat's ears and nipples as proofs of resemblance to the beasts of land ("Auribus et mammis se Quadrupedem simulabat"), though the specific reference to the cat is apparently an addition of the Old French adapter.

7. This fable is an excellent example of the ubiquity that much of this venerable material has enjoyed over the centuries, often showing up in the folklore of the most unexpected places. One finds the same basic story of the duplicitous bat exploiting its bird-like and beast-like ambivalence—though differing in detail and elaboration—in a folktale of West Africa. (See George T. Basden, *Among the Ibos of Nigeria* [London, 1921 and New York, 1966], pp. 281–82.) It is tempting to hypothesize transmission via the Arabs.

THE ASS THAT PLAYED THE HOUND

Uns homs fu qui un asne avoit
Qui sa besoigne li faisoit,
Et si estoit batus souvent,
Ne autre louier n'en avoit
Fors les chardons que il mangoit,
Dont il avoit escharsement.

Un jour se jut en son estable
Et n'ot estrain, chardons ne paille.
Son maistre esgarda qui mangoit:
Le pain vit et la char qu'il taille,
Qu'il tent a son chien et li baille,
Quant en l'espaule le feroit.

Il s'apensa que il n'avoit
Fors tourment de ce qu'il faisoit,
Et le chienet ert si a aise
Pour la joie que il menoit
Et pour l'amour que il moustroit
A son maistre et a sa maistresse.

Il pensa que aussi fera
Et que son maistre jouira,
Pour savoir se il l'ameroit;
Des piés encontre lui saudra
Et en l'oÿe le ferra,
Aussit comme le chien faisoit.

Il vit qu'il n'iert de riens tenu,
A son maistre est errant venu,

Des piés devant l'a acolé;
Puis l'a en l'ouïe feru
Du pié destre, qui ferré fu,
A pou qu'il ne l'a afollé.

Aus dens l'a par l'espaule pris,
Et estraint et a terre mis,
Sus le ventre li est monté;
Et quant ce virent ses amis,
Ses sergans, sa fame et ses fis,
L'asne ont batu et tempesté.

Il cuident qu'il soit foursené;
Liié l'ont et enchaainé
Si que il ne se puet bougier.
Or est l'asne mal asené,
Car batu est et mal mené
Et si n'a que il puist mangier.

Celui est fol a ensïent
Qui de ce qui ne li apent
S'entremet ne fait prinsautier,
Comme l'asne qui folement—
Dont il chaï en grant tourment—
Vout tolir au chien son mestier.

A cruel paterfamilias
Was wont to beat the silly ass
That toiled about his habitat.
The poor beast had to live, alas,
On little more than thorns and
    grass—
And not so very much of that!

From stable, where he lay, ill fed,
He saw the table amply spread
With food to feed our crass
    householder;
And saw his hound fed meat and
    bread
Each time that clever quadruped
Reared up and pawed his master's
    shoulder.

"How different," thought the ass,
    "from me,
Whose life is but one long ennui.
My lot, alas, is sheer disaster!
Why shouldn't I be just as free
To lavish love and bonhomie
Upon my mistress and my master?"

"Well now," he thought, "if I
    embrace
My master too, I'll find a place
In his affection, I'll be bound!
I'll up and jump with no less grace,
And with my hooves caress his face
As nicely as that silly hound!"

So, seeing that he had not been tied,
He trotted up with sprightly stride,

Flung ironed hooves round master's
    neck,
And boxed his head from side to side.
The poor man stood there, petrified—
A dumb, benumbed, bewildered
    wreck.

Beast presses on, to man's chagrin,
Kissing and hugging, chin to chin—
He bites... Man falls... Ass jumps
    upon him...
Forthwith his minions, kith and kin
Espy the ass, come running in,
And rain their clubs and cudgels on
    him.

Thinking the ass has lost his mind,
They take stout rope and chain, and
    bind
The hopeless beast—now bruised and
    sore—
Beat him before, beside, behind...
And leave him, who was so inclined
To eat in style, to eat no more.

Mad is the man whose heart is bent
On feats for which he was not meant.
Failure awaits: he won't elude it.
Witness our ass, who underwent
Tortures untold when, malcontent,
The booby played the hound, and
    rued it!

the sheep that betrayed their guardian dog to the wolves

Les leus furent en une lande,
Souffraiteus forment de viande;
Si tracent tant qu'il ont veü
Une bercherie mont grande:
Ore a chascuns ce qu'il demande;
De courre a eulz sont esmeü.

Les chiens qui les brebis gardoient
Si virent que les leus voloient
Mangier et tuer les brebis;
Du grant mautalent qu'il avoient,
Les chiens contre les leus chaploient,
Tant que les leus s'en sont fouïs.

Or oiiés que les leus feront:
Par traïson se vengeront
Des chiens qu'il ne peuent amer;
Et puis les brebis mangeront
Si que ja une n'en lairont,
Pour tant qu'il la puissent trouver.

Dont ont les leus fait assavoir
Aus brebis, s'il vuelent avoir
Pais a eulz en toute leur vie,
Les chiens leur facent faire avoir,
Que faire en puissent leur voloir,
Car vers eulz ont grant felounie.

Les brebis s'esjouirent mont
De la requeste que il ont.
Les chiens leur ont abandounés,
Puis les moustrent la ou il sont,
Ou il se dorment en un mont:
Erramment furent devorés.

Or peuent prendre les brebis,
Car ja n'en seront contredis:
Mort sont leur chiens et leur vaignons.
Tous ceulz sont folz et maubaillis
Qui baillent a leur anemis
Leur espees ne leur bastons.

Vous poués bien cest exsemplaire,
Oiant sages et folz, retraire.
Celui est fol qui sa deffense
Abandoune a son adversaire:
Bien en porroit a mal chief traire.
Qui mestier en a, si i pense!

A pack of hungry wolves were out
Prowling the country roundabout.
At length they spy a sheepfold,
　　eye it,
Eager to pounce... Now, little doubt,
No longer need they go without
The joys of this, their favorite diet.

The dogs, whose job it was to keep
A watchful eye upon the sheep,
Saw that the wolves were bent on
　　eating!
Loathing their kind, they lunge and
　　leap:
With pounding, pummeling paws
　　they heap
Their blows... Their foes desist,
　　retreating.

But listen to me and you will learn
How, treacherously, the wolves in
　　turn
Will wreak revenge; and how,
　　undone,
Those tender sheep for whom they
　　yearn—
Objects of their unique concern—
Will be devoured, each blessed one!

The wolves devise a plan. They send
Word to the sheep that they may
　　spend
Their lives in peace, no more
　　molested,

So long as they agree to lend
A hand, and help them apprehend
Those nasty dogs—despised,
　　detested.

With sheer delight the sheep believe
This guarantee (oh, how naïve!),
Tell where the dogs—to their
　　chagrin—
Lie fast asleep... Now no reprieve!
Before one tongue can shout
　　"*qui vive?*",
The wolves swoop down and do
　　them in.

And so the senseless sheep must hence
Fall to the wolves' malevolence:
Dead are their guards, malapropos.
Foolish who in his innocence
Yields sword and staff—his sole
　　defense—
Into the hands of fearsome foe!

This moral tale is meant to make
Others avoid the same mistake.
Wise man and dolt alike may need it.
Don't play the sheep, for goodness'
　　sake!
Disaster rides in folly's wake...
Let all who need this warning heed it!

THE DOG THAT COVETED HIS MEAT'S REFLECTION

Un chien fu qui passoit
Un flueve et si portoit
Un quartier de mouton.
En l'yauve se miroit;
Son ombre li sambloit
Un chien de sa façon.

La char li vout tolir
Que il vit resplendir,
Si a sa geule ouverte:
La seue li chaï.
Bien puet crier: "Haï!"
Dolant fu de sa perte.

Assés de char avoit
Et l'autrui couvoitoit,

Dont il perdi sa proie.
Qui autresi feroit
S'ainsi l'en avenoit,
Chascuns en avroit joie.

Cil qui vuelt a la gent
Tolir a ensïent
Le leur et sans raison,
A trop bon droit perdroit
Le sien que il aroit,
Com le chien le mouton.

A dog, while trotting past
A river—jaws clenched fast
About a mutton quarter—
Paused at the river's side,
Thinking that he espied
His double in the water.

Eyeing the meat's reflection,
He lunged in its direction.
But all at once: "Oh, oh!..."
With jaws agape, the glutton
Cried, as his side of mutton
Plunged to the stream below.

And so, he learned greed's cost,
For what he had, he lost—

Like all who hunger after
More than is theirs, and who,
When plans go all askew,
Are jeered with leering laughter.

The man whose mind is bent
On other's wealth, intent
To add it to his store,
Will—like the greedy dog
In this, our apologue—
Lose what was his before.

the Jay that thought himself a peacock

Un gay bel et jolif
Devint lait et chaitif
Par son outrecuidance,
Car il se fourjoï
Pour ce que il oï
De lui faire loenge.

Il ot en grant despit
Tous les gays que il vit;
O eulz ne daigne aler,
O les poons se trait,
Pour ce que il cuidoit
Les poons ressambler.

Quant les poons le virent,
En grant despit le tindrent
Et le vodrent tuer:
Ses pannes li enrachent,
Et bechent et menacent
Si qu'il ne pout voler.

Aus gays est retourné
Plumez et mal mené,
Et courcié et dolant.
Il l'ont d'entre eulz osté
Et bechié et hurté
Si qu'il fu tous sanglant.

Qui ses parens renee
Pour mener grans posnee
Et pour houneur avoir,
Aucun temps revendra
Qu'il s'en repentira:
Par droit le pues savoir.

A jay, well-formed and fair,
Once lost his gracious air
Through arrogant excess;
For his conceit was stirred
By homage he had heard
Paid to his comeliness.

He scorned each fellow jay
Who chanced to pass his way.
Instead, he proudly sought
The peacocks' company,
Finding it fit, for he
Resembled them, he thought.

The peacocks, when they found him,
Angrily gathered round him
With murder in their eye.
Plucking with claw and bill,
They scratched and bit until
He could no longer fly.

Then, featherless and sore,
He sought the jays once more.
But they, deaf to his pleading,
Near tore him limb from limb,
Then turned their backs on him
And left him bruised and bleeding.

He who would cast aside
His kin with haughty pride
And grandiose intent,
Will live to see the day
When, much to his dismay,
He shall, indeed, repent.

the asp and the locksmith's file

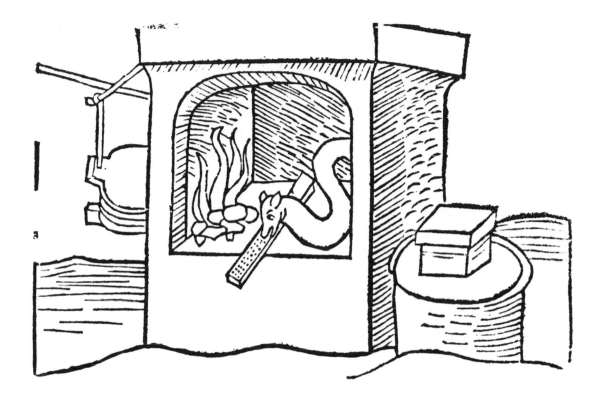

Une lime d'acier,
Chiés un serreürier,
Trouva un fol serpent.
Il la cuida mangier,
Si la prist a rungier
Trop anguoisseusement.

Ses dens sont despecies,
Rompues et brisies,
Et il fu tout sanglans.
La lime s'est moquie
De sa trés grant folie,
Et li a dit briefment:

"Fol serpent malostru,
Pour quoi me runges tu?
Dont ne sui je d'acier?
Je mangüe le fer,
S'il ert dur comme enfer,
Et tu me vuelz mangier!

Masche hardiement
Et estrain durement,
Ja ne m'en sentirai;
Tu t'en iras sanglant,
Esdenté et dolant,
Et je m'en moquerai!"

Folie est d'estriver
Et de guerre mener
A plus puissant de soi.
Qui s'en porroit garder,
Sens seroit d'eschever
La riote et le plai.

One day a hapless asp
Came on a locksmith's rasp
And set about to chew it,
Quite foolishly opining
That it would make good dining;
But he was soon to rue it.

His rash attempt, in truth,
Left not a single tooth
Unshattered in his head.
As he lay bleeding, bruised,
The rasp—amazed, amused—
Mocking his madness, said:

"You stupid asp, why try
To chew on me, when I
Myself am made of steel?
Iron is what I lunch on—
And damned tough stuff to munch
     on!—
Yet you'd make *me* your meal!

Well, chomp with jowl and jaw,
For though you gnash and gnaw
It won't hurt me a bit.
Toothless and sore, you'll beat
A bloody, bleak retreat,
And I won't care one whit!"

Folly it is to fight
When your opponent's might
Is greater than your own.
So if you prize your skin,
Before the blows begin,
Leave well enough alone.

THE BALD PEASANT AND THE FLY

Un grant vilain pelé,
Cras et bien saoulé,
Se sist a sa maison.
U haterel devant
L'ala souvent poignant
Ou vibet ou taon.

Un cop geta en vain
Le vilain, de sa main,
Sus sa teste pelee:
Malement se bleça,
La mouche n'atoucha,
Dont point ne li agree.

La mouche se traverse,
Poignant fu et diverse;
C'estoit contre sa mort.
Le vilain enticha,
Et il se courrouça.
Et li dist qu'elle a tort.

Il la cuida ferir,
Mais el seut bien fouïr
Et guenchir en volant.
Une trés grant paumee
S'est le vilain dounee
U haterel devant.

Il en jeta un ris
Et jura saint Denis

Que tant i ruëra
Qu'en aucune meniere,
Ou devant ou desriere,
A ferme la tendra.

Il la sent sus sa teste,
Si n'en fist pas grant feste,
Ains feri en soursaut;
Toute l'a escochie,
Sa teste en fu soillie
Dessus le front en haut.

Je tieng a grant folie
De faire vilounie
A plus puissant de soi:
L'an en pert bien la vie.
Sage est qui s'en chastie,
Qu'il n'en voist a besloi.
Un cop est tost rué
Et un homme tué:
Folz est qui ne se doute.
Trop enchaucer fait mal;
A pié et a cheval,
Bon fait tenir sa route.

A burly country bumpkin,
Bald as an autumn pumpkin,
Sat—in his cups—at home.
Some kind of fly, a-winging,
Time and again kept stinging
His unprotected dome.

Each time the pest would land,
The peasant smashed his hand
Smartly against his head.
Just as the bug would bite him,
He tried in vain to smite him...
But smote himself instead!

Fearing the fatal clout,
The fly buzzed round about—
Here, there and everywhere.
He stabbed, he struck, he stung...
At length the lout, unstrung,
Cursed him and cried: "Beware!

I'll get you now!" So yapping,
He recommenced his slapping,
Raining his blows unbuffered.
The bug—unthumped,
    unthwacked—
Kept coming out intact:
Only the bumpkin suffered.

With silly laugh—"Tee hee!"—
He swore by Saint Denis[8]
That he would finally smother,
Smash, mash and maul that fly,
Or know the reason why—
Some blessed way or other!

At length, when next he felt him,
He made no bones, but dealt him
Straightway one sudden smack.
The creature, crushed and shattered,
Now, at long last, lay splattered
Under his swift attack.

It's madness to persist
Against antagonist
Of greater strength and size.
Be wise or be defeated:
Desist, or you'll be treated
To premature demise.

A deadly blow, it's reckoned,
Can kill in but a second;
So why invite disaster?
Don't go beyond your speed:
Whether on foot or steed,
Go just so fast—no faster!

8. The invocation to Saint Denis, while
apparently motivated by exigencies of rhyme,
is not at all forced or out of place. As the
reputed apostle to the Gauls and first bishop
of Paris, this saint—whose existence is not
beyond question—enjoyed enormous prestige
in France throughout the Middle Ages, early
becoming the veritable patron of the royal
house. His name was a favorite in medieval
French oaths, used perhaps more frequently
than that of any other saint. (It is also
possible that the Old French translator was
playing on the saint's alleged martyrdom by
decapitation. After all, it is the peasant's head,
in the fable, that is under attack!)

"LANISTE" AND THE ANIMALS

Il eut en une lande
Une beste mont grande
Qui avoit non Laniste;
El mangoit les toriaus,
Les cers, et les chevriaus
Et les dains et les biches,

Tant que n'ot riens lessié
Que tout n'eüst mangié,
Que un tout seul torel.
Il dist en son langage:
"Ce n'est pas grand domage
Se de moi as la pel.

A bon droit nous as mors
Trestous, foibles et fors,
Car nul n'y eut aÿe.
S'au premier d'un acort
Fuissons et d'un resort,
Ne fusses or en vie.

Se toutes t'eüsson
Hurtees d'un randon,
Tu fuisses devoree.
L'une à l'autre n'aida,
Car chascune cuida
Estre plus deportee."

L'an doit l'autrui garder
Et deffendre et tenser
Aussit com soi meïsme;
Qui ainsi le feroit,
Par tant seür seroit;
Mais ici faut la rime.

A fearsome woodland beast—
The creature called Laniste[9]—
Devoured all living kind,
Filling his belly full
Of kid and stag and bull,
Of roebuck, doe and hind.

His appetite was such,
And he consumed so much,
That only one remained—
A tender bullock, who,
Seeing his turn was due,
In bovine tongue complained:

"Frankly, it matters little
If I become your victual.
We reap what we have sown:
Instead of being brothers,
Everyone let the others
Suffer their fate alone.

If only we had fought
United, as we ought,
We could have done you in.
But no! Each one believed
That he would be reprieved,
And sought to save his skin!"

It always makes good sense
To take your friend's defense
When danger comes attacking.
If everyone would do it,
We'd all come safely through it...
But here our rhyme is lacking![10]

9. I have kept the original here, since in the
Old French it is clearly intended as a proper
name, without referring to, or even suggesting,
any specific animal. Apparently it was the
author of the *Novus Æsopus* who had
transformed into this imaginary creature—
"Lanista"—the human *lanius* ("butcher") of
the fable as presented in the prose *Romulus*.
(See Léopold Hervieux, *Les Fabulistes latins
depuis le siècle d'Auguste jusqu'à la fin du
moyen âge*, 2 vols. [Paris, 1893], 2:226–67;
Georg Thiele, *Der Lateinische Äsop des
Romulus* [Heidelberg, 1910], pp. 260–61.)
10. While the last line of the original could
be understood, quite simply and prosaically,
as "But here the poem ends"—interpreting the
verb *faut* as in the celebrated close of the
Chanson de Roland, "Ci *falt* la geste que
Turoldus declinet"—such a reading would not
really present a very forceful ending to the
poet's proposed moral. I prefer to see it as a
probable pun. The poet lacks a suitable "rhyme"
just as man's behavior lacks "reason." In
other words, *ici faut la rime*, or "here's where
things fail to make sense."

THE GNAT AND THE JACKASS

Uns tahons si s'assist
Sus un mulet qu'il vit
Aler par une voie,
Qui mont chargiés estoit
D'un grant fais qu'il portoit,
Ou de cire ou de soie.

Quant vint a l'avesprer,
Si se prist a penser
Le tahon et a dire:
"Ahy, Sire Mulès!
Vous portés trop grant fès,
Je ne vous vueil plus nuire."

Il est volé arriere.
"Or estes plus ligiere,"
Fait il, "Sire Mulet!
Porté m'as longuement,
Je t'ai mont malement
Grevé et trop meffet."

Le mulet li respont:
"Tu ne poises pas mont,
Guaires ne m'as grevé;
Mon fais poise autretant
Comme il faisoit devant
Que tu fuisses levé."

Aucun cuident grever
Plus fort d'eus ou tuer,
Mais nient ne leur meffont;
Car gens de grant pooir
Et plains de grant avoir
De poi grevés ne sont.

A gadfly, out a-flitting,
Lit on a jackass, sitting
Softly and light of touch.
He spied the ponderous pack
The beast bore on his back—
Tapers or silks or such.

Soon, as the sun lay sinking,
The gadfly fell to thinking:
"Sir Ass, the way I view it,
You're loaded down enough
With all that weighty stuff.
Why must I add more to it?"

And so, he took his flight.
"There, now you're nice and light.
Forgive me if I've pained you.
Thanks to your kind assistance,
I've traveled quite a distance—
But how I must have strained you!"

At that, the jackass, snorting,
Sneered at the bug, retorting:
"Hee haw! You weightless
    midget!
My pain is far from through.
How could a mite like you
Augment it or abridge it!"

Some think that they exert
The power to do great hurt
Though they themselves are little,
Only to learn, at length,
That men of wealth and strength
Care not one jot or tittle!

ISOPET DE CHARTRES

THE MOUSE THAT WISHED
TO CROSS THE RIVER

Un souriz vout passer un fleuve,
Mès hardiesce en lui ne trueuve
Ne de passer ne fu osé.
Mout bien cuida estre arivé
Et de la reinne estre privé,
Qu'il trova delez un fossé.

Simplement li requiert aïe,
Ele ne li refuse mie,
Mès dit que bien la passera.
D'un fil l'a lié a son pié,
En sailletant l'a tant sachié,
Ja mès vif n'en eschapera.

Touz naiez sur l'eve flota;
Une escoufle les anglouta.
Mès la reinne n'i demoura;
En haut, en volant, trest la reinne

Que la souriz ot a compaingne
A ses pates, la devora.

LA SENTENCE DE LA FABLE

Bien nos enseingne ci la flabe:
Traïson oeuvre de deable.
Nus hom ne doit autre trahir;
Toute en porroit avoir la painne
Si comme ot par son laz la Reinne;
Don devons traïson haïr.

Quisquis credentem sibi prodit, proditur; ille,
Sicut Rana, suo jure perit laqueo.

A mouse desired to cross a river,
But—timorous beast, of lilyish
    liver—
Shied from the risk and dared not
    take it.
Spying a frog beside a ditch,
She thought she'd found the means
    by which—
Friends being friends—she'd surely
    make it.

And so the mouse, nice as you please,
Asks for her help. The frog agrees,
Says she'll transport her, shore to
    shore,
Ties her, secures her... Ah, but then...
Pounce! Seize! Attack!... Again,
    again...
Exit the mouse, forevermore.

Now there they are: the mouse—
    dead, floating,
Tied to the frog—and the frog,
    gloating

Over her ruse, when, then and there,
A kite swoops low, out of the blue,
Sweeps them both up, mouse and
    frog too,
Gobbles them down, right in midair.

THE MORAL OF THE FABLE

The lesson from our tale ensuing:
Treachery is the devil's doing.
Let man betray no mother's son;
He may, himself, reap all the woe,
Just like the frog who—rightly so—
Did ill and was, in turn, undone.

Betray another's trust and be betrayed,
Like Frog, who perished in the trap she laid.[11]

11. All the fables in the Chartres collection,
with one exception, reproduce—sometimes
with minor modifications—the two-line moral
tags of the Latin models in the *Novus Æsopus.*

the dog that sued the lamb

JK

Li chien qui volentiers ne baille
Son pain, se fist envers l'oaille
De prester large et charitable.
A l'ouaille revint a plain,
Si dist qu'i li rendist son pain;
Ele nia, tout tint a fable.

Devant le juge l'accusa,
Car dou rendre le refusa;
Li juges tesmoing en requiert.
Li lou, l'escoufle et l'ostoir dirent
Qu'a celle le pain prester virent
Et dient que veritez iert.

Quant le jugement entendi,
Le pain tot par force rendi;
Mout en fu corrociee et mue
Quar el nel avoit de quoi rendre:

Sa lainne li en couvint vendre,
Si remaint frileuse et nue.

LA SENTENCE DE LA FABLE

Se vos de plaidier n'estes sage,
Ne plaidiez jour de vostre aage
Sanz conseil, soiez clerc ou lai;
Car tost seriez deceü:
Rendre ce que n'avez deü
Vos convendroit tout sanz delai.

Sic tutore carens vir simplex fraude coactus
Hoc quod non habuit reddere sepe solet.

The hound—no generous creature he—
Pretended unabashedly
He'd lent the lamb a bread. Bold, brash,
He came to claim it. She demurred,
Denied the tale, called it absurd,
Said it was utter balderdash.

The hound took her to court, brought suit.
The judge found ample resolute
Witnesses for the prosecution:
Wolf, kite, hawk—one and all, they said
They'd seen the hound lend her the bread
And that she owed him restitution.

The judge pronounced his verdict: Would she
Forthwith return the bread!... How could she?

What should she do?... In her distress
She sells her fleece. There she stands, shorn,
Bare as the day that she was born,
Shaken, chagrined, cold, comfortless.

THE MORAL OF THE FABLE

If legal art is not your forte,
Never, I pray, get caught in court
Without defense. For be you lay
Or be you cleric, the law's the law...
The verdict's in—no hem, no haw:
You say you're right? You're wrong! So pay!

Oft must the artless victim, tutorless,
Yield what he never did, in truth, possess.

THE LION AND THE SHEPHERD

Un lion ou pié se bleça,
Car dedens la char li dreça
Une espine grelle et poingnant.
Au pastorel s'en vet clochant
Qu'il trova en un pré trotant;
Mout se paint et veit regroingnant.

Il li prie par amours fine
Que dou pié li oste l'espine.
Li pastor mout va reculant,
Mès li lions, sanz chiere fole,
Simplement par bele parole,
Son pié li moustra en ulant.

Li pastorel conoist la chose,
D'eïde refuser ne l'ose,
L'espine li tret par pitié,
Il l'aguille hors de son pié,
Tant que il fut et baut et lié;
Graces l'en rent et amitié.

Aprés lonc tens fu pris au piege
Celui qui les bestes assiege
Et fu mené vendre au marchié;
Tantost avint de cop en paume
Que li pastors fut pris por blame,
Mont fu des gens mal decachié.

Livré l'ont au bestes sauvages;
Mès li lions fu fiers et sages,

Bien le connoist, si court a lui;
Il s'areste, les mains li leiche,
Vers lui n'est pas de male teiche
Ne n'iert irez ne empaliz.

Des bestes tout le deffendi.
Quant li puepies ce entendi,
Au pastorel vont tuit parler
Demandans que ce puet monter;
Quant tot ot pris a raconter,
Par pitié le lessent aler.

LA SENTENCE DE LA FABLE

Bien devons avoir en memoire
Noz biensfetours, s'en male foire
Les verrons maumestre et perir;
Tout nos devons abandonner
Dou bienfet tout guerredonner
Selonc le pooir dou merir.

Hic collatorum memores nos esse bonorum
Ammonet et laeta mente referre vicem.

138

A lion, wounded, lay forlorn:
Stuck in his paw, a painful thorn.
He spied a shepherd-boy close by him,
And moaning many a "welladay"
And "woe is me," he limped his way
As best he could, and soon drew nigh
    him.

Meekly he begs the shepherd's aid
In pulling out the thorn. Afraid,
The young man jumps, shrinks back.
    Again
The beast entreats, with mournful air
Repeats his humble, piteous prayer,
Holds up his paw and howls his pain.

The shepherd understands, dares not
Deny the help the beast has sought.
Touched by his plight, our thorn-
    extractor
Pricks at the culprit, pulls... *Voilà*!
The lion heaves a heartfelt "ah,"
And heaps thanks on his benefactor.

Years pass. The fearsome lion falls
    victim:
Those who sell beasts for sport have
    tricked him,
Trapped him. The Games are now his
    lot.
By chance, just so, the shepherd too
Has run afoul, condemned to do

What Justice dictates, just or not.[12]
They throw him to the beasts.
    However,
Our friend the lion, canny and clever,
Knows him at once—no "buts,"
    "ifs," "ands"—
Runs to his side, poised, calm,
    controlled...
Stops, looks... And then... Lo and
    behold!
Gently he licks the prisoner's hands!

Woe be to any beast who dare
Attack this man!... The people stare
In awe and disbelief. They hail
Him, ply him with their "hows" and
    "whys"...
He tells his tale... They sympathize,
And free him from his harsh travail.[13]

12. The Old French original is a trifle murky here, as is frequently the case with the overly terse Chartres fables. I have taken the liberty of clarifying and expanding slightly on the text, on the basis of the corresponding passage in the *Novus Æsopus*: "Longo post tempore, captus, / Ad Theatri ludos venditur ipse Leo. / Pastor erat per tempus idem pro crimine captus; / Damnatus theatri traditur ille feris."
13. Readers will easily recognize here a version of the Androcles story, the Greek original of which dates back only to the first century A.D., in Apion's *Aiguptiaka*, and is considerably post-Æsopic.

THE MORAL OF THE FABLE

When thoughtful soul befriends
    us, we
Should not forget his charity
In latter, darker days: to wit,
When he himself, in turn, lies low.[14]
Pay him with generous *quid pro quo*:
Favor for favor, tat for tit.

Thus are we taught to bear good deeds in mind:
Kindness should always be repaid in kind.[15]

14. The exact sense of the original *s'en male foire* is debatable at best. Godefroy's authoritative *Dictionnaire de l'ancienne langue française* cites it under *foire*, but with the very different (and, to my mind, less than plausible) reading of *sanz male foire*, giving the meaning of *retour, réciprocité* ("return," "reciprocity") for that noun. I assume, at least, that my translation preserves the general, if not the specific, intent.

15. Our fabulist—or scribe—appears to have misread as *hic* an original *hoc* in the *Novus Æsopus*: "Hoc collatorum memores . . ."

the sick ass and the wolf physician

Une asne se gisoit a terre.
Li lou vint a lui tout sanz guerre,
Au dens soement le gratoit.
Cil demande, qui mout set d'art,
Ou plus se deult et en quel part.
Il dit que la ou il tastoit.

LA SENTENCE DE LA FABLE

Ainsit est, qui bien i avise,
S'aucun aloit nuz en chemise

Jeünant en pelerinage,
Por qu'il soit des gens diffamez
Ne sara il ja mès amez
N'apelé bon tout son aage.

Vir sic infidus videtur, quum officiosus:
  Cum facit ipse bonum, creditur esse malum.

An ass, in pain, lay on the ground,
The wolf, meaning no harm, came
 round,
Nuzzled her gently here and there
With probing tooth, and, amply
 versed
In physic, asked where it hurt the
 worst.
"Right where your teeth are, wolf,
 that's where!"

THE MORAL OF THE FABLE

Mark well the tale, for so it goes.
Such are the ways and such the woes

Of ill repute. Beware ill fame:
You can go threadbare—naked
 nearly—
Visit the shrines, pray, fast austerely...
Nothing you do will clear your name.

Let man appear the knave: his every action,
Fair though it be, will seem foul malefaction.[16]

16. For reasons not easy to determine, our
fabulist has altered the first line of the moral
tag of his *Novus Æsopus* model: "Vir sic
infidus, fit quislibet officiosus..." Perhaps he
found the original too categorical and chose to
soften the portrait somewhat ("Vir sic
infidus *videtur*..."). Or perhaps he was using
as his text a lost variant. Then too, there is
always the possibility of scribal error or
intentional license when dealing with such
venerable texts.

the horse and the lion physician

Un lion vit pestre un cheval
En un vert pré tout contreval:
A lui vint, si li print a dire
Qu'il guerist plaies et gouverne
Mielz que nul mire de Salerne;
Mout se fet de plaies bon mire.

Le cheval voit bien sa boidie,
Que cil li veut tollir la vie;
Il lesse a pestre acoardiz,
Mès il li dist: "Biau douz amis,
Bien voi que ci t'a Dieu tramis."
Si se feint et fet le hardiz.

"L'autre jour ou pié me feri
Une espine, onc puis ne gueri;
Mès trop es bon cyrurgïen;
Se Dieu plest, bien me gueriras."
Il li a dit: "Tu sentiras
Coment je te gueriré bien."

Quant il le vout ou pié taster,
Le cheval nou seufre a grater;
En la teste le va ferir
Des .II. piez si qu'il l'abati.

Mout l'escarnist quant l'ot flati,
Si li a dit c'or puet guerir.

Li cheval tantost s'em parti,
Car dou jeu ot trop mieuz parti.
Li lion dit: "C'est a droiture;
Or ne me pris ge une escorce
Quant desus lui avoie force
Et d'estre mire avoie cure."

LA SENTENCE DE LA FABLE

De ceste fable est la somme
Que gentil hom ne doit son home
Prendre par barat ne par guille.
Se honte n'en a, bien puet dire,
Que de son barat a le pire
Et la queue tient de l'anguille.

Nobilis ad turpes quum non verti pudet artes,
Formidet turpi se quoque fraude capi.

A lion on the prowl stood gazing:
There, on the grass, a horse was
　　grazing!
Lion approaches... Draws abreast...
Proclaims himself a doctor rare,
Physician *extraordinaire*,
Better than all Salerno's best.[17]

Horse stops his browsing... Not much
　　doubt
Just what the vicious beast's about:
Alas for life and limb! Atremble,
Cringing, he neighs: "Dear, gentle
　　friend,[18] you
Come just in time! Did Heaven send
　　you?"
(What dare he do?... Be bold,
　　dissemble...)

"Speaking of doctors, *à propos*,
I pricked my hoof not long ago
But nothing helps. I'll let you see it.
God willing you can find the cure!"
"For sure," the lion sneers, "for sure!
I'll fix you up, I guarantee it!"

Just as the lion plots his moves,
The horse rears up, lifts both front
　　hooves
And brings them crashing with a
　　"pow!"
Down on his head, surefootedly,
Laying the lion low. "Dear me,"
He smirks, "it feels much better
　　now!"

The horse goes trotting off, content
With his unique accomplishment.
The lion groans, moans: "Oh la la,
It serves me right, I'm such a twit!
I was ahead... I should have quit!
Me and my stories! Doctors! Bah!"

THE MORAL OF THE FABLE

The essence of our tale is that
One should observe this caveat:
He who plays false and underhanded,
Shameless, deserves the fate he earns.
Fraud begets fraud... The table turns...
He's sure to lose the fish he's landed.[19]

Let gentle lord all shameful wiles eschew,
Or fear lest wiles as base undo him too![20]

17. Salerno was celebrated for its school of
medicine as early as the ninth century, and
remained so throughout the Middle Ages.
18. The phrase *biau douz amis* had, by this
time, become a veritable cliché in Old French
letters. Its use here, obviously, underlines the
horse's self-defensive sycophantism.
19. The last line of the original alludes to an
Old French proverb, traceable at least to the
13th century: "Qui tient l'anguille par la cue
Il ne l'a mie"; literally, "He who holds the
eel by the tail doesn't hold it at all." (See Le
Roux de Lincy, I: 91. Joseph Morawski,
Proverbes français antérieurs au XVe siècle
[Paris, 1925], no. 2159, cites the same proverb
with minor variations.)
20. The first line of the *Novus Æsopus* tag
reads somewhat differently: "Nobilis ad turpes
verti quem non pudet artes..."

the horse that wished to hunt the stag

Un cheval qui fu grant et fort
Un cerf haoit a desconfort;
Mout fu iriez, pensiz et morne;
Vaintre nou poit pour point qu'il face,
Ne par force ne par menace,
Car bien est armez de ses cornes.

Le chaceor requiert et prie,
Qui tant o ses chiens chace et guie,
Que il puisse prendre le cerf.
Si li a dit que plus n'areste,
Le frain et la sele li meste:
Tant que il soit pris, sera serf.

Mout li plest ce qu'il ot conter,
Sor le cheval prist a monter,
Le cerf chacierent par le bois.
Le cerf qui ne fu pas chargié
Ot de corre meillor marchié,
Si eschapa tout en gabois.

Li cheval ot coru assez,
Dou fès de l'ome fu lassez.
Mout li prie que il descende,
Car bien voudroit estre delivre
Et ausi comme devant vivre,
Car cheval d'achacier n'amende.

Cil dit: "Tu t'ies moult mal vanté.
Sur toi sui par ta volenté,
Or me serf donc com ton seigneur."
Son frain commença a rungier,
L'ome cuida soz lui plungier,
Mès n'ot pas la force greigneur.

Cil le feroit d'un bleceron
Sor la croupe et de l'esperon.
Sa maniere li fist muer,
Si que maugré suen le servi,
Car il ot mout bien deservi,
Onc puis ne se vout remuer.

LA SENTENCE DE LA FABLE

Por ce poez avoir fiance
Que qui couvoite grant venchance
D'autrui, sanz atremper corage,
Bien gart lui meïsmes ne grieve,
Car tel chiet qui puis ne se lieve
Et s'aperçoit de son outrage.

Quisquis vindictam nimiam cupit, audiat ista
Ne, dum vult hostem perdere, se perimat.

A horse there was who roundly
    hated
A certain stag—nay, execrated!
Powerful though he was, the horse
Was no match for his antlered foe.
Alas, alack, no luck! And so:
Retreat, regret... but no recourse.

No, none... That is, until he meets
Hunter and hounds... Asks, begs,
    entreats:
"Please, help me bag the stag!"
    "Indeed,"
The hunter cries... Fits bit and saddle
Onto the horse, jumps up astraddle...
"And you can be my trusty steed!"

Up and away! And through the wood
They chased the stag as best they
    could.
But all to no avail: stout-hearted
Stag gallops free, unmanned,
    unmounted—
Unlike our horse—and that's what
    counted.
"Pish tush!" he jeered, and off he
    darted.

The horse, with many a huff and puff,
Soon realized he'd run enough.
His mount weighed heavy... "Sire, I
    pray you,

Get off my back and let me be.
That stag is just too fast for me.
Please, sire, get off... You hear?...
    What say you?"

"Pshaw, my fine friend!" the hunter
    said.
"I'm here to stay! You made your bed!
From now on I'm your lord and
    master!"
Frantic, the horse chafes, champs,
    jumps, jerks,
Rears, tries to throw him... Nothing
    works.
Too late... Too weak... Despair...
    Disaster!

Hunter, at length, with spur and
    whip,[21]
Confirms the new relationship
'Twixt him and horse. Now bruised
    and sore,
The latter, loath, accepts what is,
Alas, his lot! The fault is his.
He's learned his lesson... Nevermore!

21. While the exact meaning of the noun
bleceron is, to the best of my knowledge,
unattested elsewhere in Old French literature,
the sense of the original seems clear. The Latin
of the *Novus Æsopus* makes it doubly so:
"'... flagellis / Nolentem cogam te mea
jussa sequi.'"

THE MORAL OF THE FABLE

He who seeks vengeance past all
    measure
Soon may, himself, repent at leisure.
Hark to the truth our tale professes!
Mark well the message: Many's the
    man
Who ends much worse than he began,
Sad victim of his own excesses.

Fie, you who crave revenge more than one ought:
Well may you perish, whilst your foe may not![22]

22. Our fabulist has changed (or misread) a
capit in the Latin tag of the *Novus Æsopus* as
cupit ("Quisquis vindictam nimiam cupit . . .").
The meaning is not seriously altered, though
not everyone who yearns for (*cupit*) revenge
necessarily takes (*capit*) it.

THE ANT AND THE CRICKET

Oez la fable dou fromi
Qui en esté n'est endormi:
Mout est de grant porchaz et sage,
Car tout esté desque en yver
Conquiert qu'il menjue l'yver;
Ce n'est pas mauvès vaselage.

En ce tens qu'il fist grant froidure,
S'en vint a lui, par aventure,
Toz afamez, un gresillon;
De fain a soufert grant torment,
Si demande de son froment.
"Grant tens a ne sui fornillon."

Li fromi li a respondu,
"Bien me resembles fol tondu!
Porquoi n'en as tu porchacié?"
Il li a dit: "Touz jourz chantoie
Sanz reposer, ne ne pouoie
Estre de ces jardins chacié."

Li fromi dit: "Sire enchanté,
En esté avez bien chanté.
Or poez en l'iver saillir.
Autre froment alez lober!
Or poez morir ou rober,
Si voz porroiz bien maubaillir."

LA SENTENCE DE LA FABLE

La fable nos veut exposer
Que cil ne se font aloser
Qui sont vains et plains de paresce.
En esté doivent labourer
Pour eus en yver ennourer,
Que la meseise ne le blesce.

Ammonet haec pigros estate vacare labori
Ne mendicantes frigore nil capiant.

Listen now to the tale about
The ant who toiled, day in day out,
All summer long, untiringly,
Working and working, harder and
    harder,
Storing away his winter larder:
Provident, prudent creature he![23]
Now then, by chance, one winter's
    day—
Cold as could be—there passed his
    way
A hungry cricket... Hungry? No,
Famished, more nearly, blithely come
A-begging: "Please! A crust... A
    crumb...
I have no bread! Weeks, months ago,

I didn't bake one blessèd loaf!"
The ant replied: "You silly oaf!
You're not like me! Who told you
    not to?"
Cricket: "Good sir, I beg your pardon!
All day I sang in yonder garden,
Exactly as I thought I ought to."

Answered the ant: "Well, songster
    friend![24]
You sang all summer? Good! now
    spend
The winter dancing! Fie! For shame!
You'll have to find some other dupe!
Starve or go steal, poor nincompoop!
You only have yourself to blame!"

THE MORAL OF THE FABLE

Idleness, so this fable proves,
Badly befits and ill behooves
Those who would earn our
    admiration.
Summertime, let them labor, lest
The winter find them sore distressed:
No work, no food!... No food,
    starvation![25]

Be not a summer idler, labor spurning;
Else be a winter beggar, nothing earning.

23. Readers will notice that I have followed
the original here, respecting the grammatical
gender of the Old French *fromi*—and,
subsequently, *gresillon*—despite the temptation
to echo the celebrated version of La Fontaine,
for whom the nouns *fourmi* and *cigale* dictated
feminization of the characters: "La Cigale,
ayant chanté / Tout l'été, / Se trouva fort
dépourvue / Quand la bise fut venue: / Pas
un seul petit morceau / De mouche ou de
vermisseau. / Elle alla crier famine / Chez la
Fourmi sa voisine..."
24. The original *enchanté*, "one who sings,"
would appear to be a pun. At any rate, it seems
to be an unusual, if not solitary, usage. The
Godefroy *Dictionnaire* cites only the present
passage as an example.
25. Like much of the vocabulary in the
Chartres manuscript, the meaning of the verb
ennourer is debatable. Godefroy suggests
"nourish," basing the assumption on the passage
here translated, apparently the only one extant
in which the word is used.

Notes
Selected Bibliography

Notes

1. Aside from the well-studied texts of the whole range of Asiatic and Mediterranean cultures from Japan and China to Greece and beyond, traditions that have remained oral until far more recently, African, American Indian, and Polynesian, all have animal tales handed on from generation to generation. See, for instance, *African Myths and Tales*, ed. Susan Feldmann (New York: Dell, 1963); for Polynesian examples, Rolf Kuschel: *Animal Stories from Bellona Island* (Glydendal: National Museum of Denmark, 1975); and for an overview of motifs in many cultures, from the Japanese and Malaysian to the American Indian, Antti Amatus Aarne, *Die Tiere auf der wanderschaft, eine märchenstudie* (Hamina, Finland: Suomalaisen tiedeakatemian kustantama, 1913).

2. Henri Frankfort, *The Arts and Architecture of the Ancient Orient* (Baltimore: Penguin Books, 1955), *Figure* 38 (description and discussion, p. 35).

3. Ibid.

4. In *Babrius and Phaedrus*, ed. Ben Edwin Perry (London: W. Heinemann, and Cambridge, Mass.: Harvard University Press, 1965), xix–xx.

5. Ibid., xi, xx.

6. Ibid., pp. 254–255.

7. These words are not really interchangeable, even though they are true cognates, and both carry such modern meanings as "adage," "simile," and "proverb." The Arabic word (but not the Hebrew) can also mean "likeness." Perry is possibly right to identify them with "what we call a proverb" (Perry, *Babrius and Phaedrus*, xx); but the type of statement illustrated by the eponymously titled Hebrew Book of *Proverbs* (*Mishlei*) is more prescriptive than descriptive, more philosophical than practical.

8. *II Samuel* 12, 1–7; also cited by Perry, *Babrius and Phaedrus*, xxii. Nathan the Prophet has been sent by the Lord to excoriate King David for his crime against Uriah, Bathsheba's husband. Nathan's parable of a rich man that passes over all his own flocks to seize a poor man's only ewe lamb to prepare for his guest incenses David against its subject and invites the response already quoted.

9. An important exception is *Kalīla waDimna*, an eighth-century Arabic translation of a Syriac or Persian "original" (itself conjectured to be a translation of the fourth-century Sanskrit *Panchatantra*). Kalīla and Dimna are the names of two jackals that figure in the framing story, and narrate the others that it contains (see the editions of Antoine Isaac Silvestre de Sacy, Paris: de l'Imprimerie royale, 1816, and Joseph Derenbourg, Paris: F. Vieweg, 1887–89).

10. August Hausrath, "Achiqar und Aesop: das Verhältnis der orientalischen zur griechischen Fabeldichtung," in *Sitzungsberichte der Heidelberger Akademie der Wissenschaften*, Heidelberg: C. Winter, 1918, p. 3.

11. This basic story descends through the *Panchatantra* and its derivatives into that of the so-called Seven Sages of Rome, of which there are versions in Latin and virtually every medieval European language.

12. *Hitopadeśa. The Book of Wholesome Counsel*, tr. Francis Johnson, rev. and ed. Lionel D. Barnett (London: Chapman and Hall, Ltd., 1928).

13. Edited by Perry, *Aesopica*, Volume I (Urbana: University of Illinois Press, 1952), pp. 81–130. Perry published the two major Greek versions, and one Latin version.

14. Hausrath, "Achiqar und Aesop," p. 45.

15. See, for example, S. N. Kramer, *History Begins at Sumer* (Garden City, New York: Doubleday and Co., 1959), Chapter 17, for numerous apposite citations from Akkadian clay tablets almost 4000 years old.

16. It is Aesop's disdain for the Delphians, after he discovers how far short of their reputation they fall, that arouses their anger and lust for revenge. Interestingly, they use the device of Joseph against his brothers, hiding a gold cup in Aesop's baggage so that they can inculpate him for theft and condemn him to death. See the account in the *Life of Aesop*, sections 124–128, in Perry, *Aesopica*, volume I, pp. 104–105.

17. Aesop does not appear to have been one. But Perry, seeking an explanation for the fact that Aesop, historically a Thracian, entered and has remained in legend a Phrygian, mentions the conjecture that he was refashioned in imitation of the Phrygian musician Marsyas. This was a rustic cultural hero who challenged Apollo to a musical contest and was (unsurprisingly) defeated (*Babrius and Phaedrus*, xxxv–xxxvi, xl–xlii).

18. Only indirect sources, however. As Julia Bastin writes (*Recueil général des Isopets*, 2 vols., Paris: Librairie ancienne Honoré Champion, 1929: I, ii): "Pendant tout le moyen âge, Phèdre n'a guère été connu, et, à partir d'une certaine époque, n'a plus été connu que par des rédactions dérivées qui avaient pour base des manuscrits aujourd'hui perdus et plus complets que ceux que nous possédons."

19. Said to have been a characteristic of the so-called sybaritic fable. See, for example, *Ésope: Fables*, ed. Émile Chambry (Paris: Société d'édition "Les belles lettres," 1927), xxiv: "Le scholiaste d'Aristophane (*Oiseaux*, 471) prétend que les fables ésopiques se distinguent des sybaritiques en ce que, dans les premières, les personnages sont des animaux, dans les secondes, des hommes. . . ."

20. The extraordinary utopian vision of *Babrius* 102 (ed. Perry, p. 131), in which an enlightened lion ruler allows the weak to call the strong to account, is a striking exception to this, and to what is noted above about the relation of strong and weak.

21. See also Perry, *Babrius and Phaedrus*, Appendix, No. 91, pp. 438–439, for another version. Apuleius's sophisticated satire *The Golden Ass* incorporates many amusing variants on the difficulties of expressing emotions pleasing to human beings through the body of an ass. A similar fable is *Babrius* 125, of the ass capering on the roof tiles in imitation of an ape.

22. A macabre reworking of the idea of this fable is in the episode that gives its title to Jerzy Kosinski's book *The Painted Bird*. See also *Babrius* 72, of the daw whose plumage borrowed from all the other birds almost deceived Zeus into awarding it a prize for beauty.

23. The fable is mentioned in Aristotle's *Rhetoric* II, 20 (where the horse is immediately subjected by its rider, before undertaking the projected hunt); see also *Chartres* 23. The unfortunate horse's final situation may suggest that of the sailor Sinbad with the Old Man of the Sea clinging to his shoulders and "riding" him where he willed (see *The Thousand and One Nights*, tr. E. W. Lane, 3 vols., London: Chatto and Windus, 1883), vol. III, pp. 51–55.

24. In both the prose *Babrius* and the prose *Phaedrus*. See also *Chartres* 5. Dante applies this fable to a situation in which a fallen angel, plotting the misfortune of another, brings them both to disaster (*Inferno* XXII, 118–XXIII, 9).

25. La Fontaine puts the point succinctly in the opening line of his version (V, xiii): "L'avarice perd tout en voulant tout gagner."

26. Readers will remember this as the plight of Winnie the Pooh after he overeats in Rabbit's house and finds he can no longer pass through the hole by which he entered (*Winnie the Pooh*, Chapter 2: "In which Pooh goes visiting and gets into a tight place").

27. *Agamemnon*, v. 177. The phrase is usually translated, *wisdom* (or *understanding*) *through suffering*.

28. See Francis Klingender, *Animals in Art and Thought to the End of the Middle Ages* (Cambridge, Mass.: The M.I.T. Press, 1971), pp. 92–94.

29. Also noted ibid., p. 360.

30. On all this, see Urban T. Holmes, Jr., *A History of Old French Literature from the Origins to 1300*, rev. ed. (New York: Russell and Russell, 1962), pp. 207–210.

31. In *Marie de France: An Analytical Bibliography*, by Glyn S. Burgess (London: Grant and Cutler, 1977), the vast majority of some five hundred items listed (including dissertations) are concerned with the *Lays*; no more than a couple of dozen deal specifically with the *Fables*. The *Lays* can now be read in their entirety in a new English prose translation by Robert Hanning and Joan Ferrante: *The Lais of Marie de France* (New York: Dutton, 1978).

32. They are extensively canvassed in Richard Baum, *Recherches sur les oeuvres attribuées à Marie de France* (Heidelberg: C. Winter, 1968); see also Emanuel J. Mickle, Jr., *Marie de France* (New York: Twayne, 1974).

33. These manuscripts are listed in Burgess.

34. See Bastin, I, ix–x, xiii–xiv, xxi–xxii; II, iv–v. Bastin considers the work of Walter the Englishman to be the source of *Isopet I*.

35. For an interesting discussion of the role of Marie's fables as possible precursors or parallels of these cycles, see Chapter 1 of Hans Robert Jauss's *Untersuchungen zur mittelalterlichen Tierdichtung* (Tübingen: M. Niemeyer, 1959). On the other hand, Holmes, *Old French Literature*, p. 211, holds that the *Roman de Renart* ". . . is entirely distinct from the fable."

36. A *fabliau* is a satirical tale (in verse or prose) of social or sexual mores, often scabrous in its details and pungent in its wit. It is typically much longer than the fable. *Fabliaux* abound in both the Latin and vernacular literature of the high Middle Ages, and formed the basis of tales by late medieval authors such as Chaucer (in *The Miller's Tale* and *The Reeve's Tale*, for instance) and Boccaccio.

37. The text in the mass is *Agnus Dei, qui tollis peccata mundi* (Lamb of God, who takest away the sins of the world). The lamb that the wolf intends to eat will "take away" his sin in eating it by "becoming" a salmon.

38. This may be reminiscent of the situation in the Psalm of Babylonian captivity (No. 137): "They said, Sing us a song of Zion. . . . How can we sing the Lord's song in a strange land?"

39. This is a quite literal rendering of "*Ceo que jeo t'oi . . . preié, | Dunt tu m'aveies manacié*," reading *dunt* as "with which" to suggest that the fox is thinking specifically of giving the bear a "beating with his stick." On the other hand, *dunt* may well mean here, "on account of which." Marie's editor Karl Warnke (*Die Fabeln der Marie de France*, Halle: W. Niemeyer, 1898, p. 388), seems to allow both senses here (*wovon*; *womit*), though his other meanings (*wodurch*; *wofür*, *weshalb*) suggest that he is everywhere thinking of cause rather than specification.

40. The most famous poem of the turn of the twelfth century, and one of the earliest extant in French, *La chanson de Roland*, is still characterized by assonance, rather than rhyme—though rhyme had appeared somewhat earlier in Latin poetry. See F. J. E. Raby, *Secular Latin Poetry* (2 vols., Oxford: Oxford University Press, 1934; 2nd edition, 1957); and Fred Brittain, *The Medieval Latin and Romance Lyric to A.D. 1300*, 2nd edition (Cambridge: Cambridge University Press, 1951).

41. The typical medieval hierarchy of treachery given by Dante makes betrayal of benefactors the worst, after treachery to relatives (one's own "kind"), country, and friends.

42. This is a common metric of the *Isopet II* poet, and characterizes all the remaining fables of his that are included in the present volume.

43. Apuleius's second-century novel *Metamorphoses* (more popularly known as *The Golden Ass*) offers numerous instances.

44. For a discussion of the technical meanings of the phrase *fin'amors* in

chivalric romance and troubadour poetry, see Moshe Lazar, *Amour courtois et fin'amors dans la littérature du douzième siècle* (Paris: Librairie C. Klincksieck, 1964).

45. For a Shakespearean use of a very similar motif, see *The Winter's Tale* III, ii, 208–214.

46. Luigi Pirandello's short story *La patente* (*The License*), and the one-act play derived from it, offer a very different treatment of the same theme: the invincible power of an evil reputation.

47. For a vivid and entertaining view of the life of a poet and his view of patronage towards the end of the twelfth century, see the famous anonymous poem known as the "Goliard's Confession" (printed in many anthologies of medieval Latin verse). Another poem about patronage, dating from the mid-thirteenth century, is Colin Muset's "Sire cuens, j'ai vielé," translated by Norman Shapiro in *An Anthology of Medieval Lyrics*, ed. Angel Flores (New York: Modern Library, 1962), pp. 138–140.

48. There is a remarkable efflorescence of satirical Aesopica in the form of pro- and anti-monarchical and other political writings published (anonymously, of course) around the turn of the eighteenth century. The titles mostly have the form *Aesop at . . .*, e.g., *Aesop at Bathe, Aesop at Tunbridge, Aesop at Whitehal* (all 1698), and a reply to them dated to the same year, *Aesop at Amsterdam.* There is even an *Aesop Junior in America*, dated 1834.

Selected Bibliography

I: Manuscripts

1. *Marie de France*

For a listing of the twenty-three manuscripts of Marie's *Fables*, please refer to Burgess's *Analytical Bibliography* (see Section III, below), pp. 11–13.

2. *Isopet I*

A. Brussels, *Bibliothèque royale de Belgique*, 11193. There are 132 folios, containing sixty-four fables with Prologue and Epilogue, as well as the nineteen fables of *Avionnet* with their Prologue and Epilogue. Texts in both Latin and French, illuminated with miniatures. Bastin does not state the date of this manuscript.

B. Paris, *Bibliothèque nationale*, fr. 1594. There are 113 folios, with the same contents as the Brussels MS, and miniature illuminations. Probably fourteenth century.

C. London, *British Museum*, Add. Mss. 33781. A small quarto, with 132 folios containing the same texts as the two previous manuscripts. The calligraphy is most likely French and of the fourteenth century. There are eighty-three miniatures.

D. Paris, *Bibliothèque nationale*, fr. 1595. Thirty-eight folios, containing *Isopet I* in French only, with another work in part. Fifteenth century.

E. Paris, *Bibliothèque nationale*, fr. 19123. The fables of *Isopet I* and *Avionnet* are found on folios 110 to 132. Fifteenth century, no illustrations.

F. Paris, *Bibliothèque nationale*, fr. 24310. This fifteenth-century manuscript contains, in addition to *Isopet I* and *Avionnet*, the fables of *Marie de France* (see Burgess, p. 12, item 9). There are spaces for illustrations never made.

3. *Isopet II*

A. Paris, *Bibliothèque nationale*, fr. 24432. The manuscript dates from the middle of the fourteenth century. The fables are found on folios 171 *verso* to 184. No illustrations.

B. Paris, *Bibliothèque nationale*, fr. 15213. The manuscript probably dates from the second half of the fourteenth century. The fables run from folio 1 to folio 55 *recto*, and are illustrated with numerous miniatures.

4. *Isopet de Chartres*

Bibliothèque de Chartres, 620. Probably end of the thirteenth century. The fables are on the last folios, Nos. 136 *verso* to 149 *recto*.

II: Major Editions

1. *Marie de France*

   A. Ewert, Alfred, and Ronald C. Johnston. *Marie de France: Fables.* Oxford: Blackwell, 1942. This edition contains the French text of forty-six fables and the Prologue and Epilogue, with an Introduction, Notes, and a Glossary in English.

   B. Gumbrecht, Hans U. *Marie de France: Äsop, eingeleitet, kommentiert und übersetzt.* Munich: W. Fink, 1973. Gumbrecht gives the French text of 102 fables, Prologue and Epilogue, with a bibliography, critical essay, and prose translations in German.

   C. Warnke, Karl. *Die Fabeln der Marie de France.* Halle: W. Niemeyer, 1898. Contains the French text of the Prologue, Epilogue, and one hundred and two fables with variants. There are also a comprehensive Introduction, Notes, Appendices, and an extensive Glossary in German.

2. *Isopet I, Isopet II,* and *Isopet de Chartres*

   Bastin, Julia. *Recueil général des Isopets.* Two volumes. Paris: Librairie ancienne Honoré Champion, 1929. This edition contains the French texts of all three of these collections (Prologue, Epilogue, and sixty-four fables for *Isopet I,* forty fables with Prologue and Epilogue for *Isopet II,* and the same for *Isopet de Chartres,* as well as the Latin text of the *Novus Aesopus* (forty-two fables), with an Introduction and notes on variant readings.

III: Bibliography

Burgess, Glyn S. *Marie de France: an Analytical Bibliography.* London: Grant and Cutler, 1977. This valuable book offers a comprehensive listing, with brief commentary, of the manuscripts and principal editions of Marie's works, as well as of some five hundred critical studies, articles, and dissertations. Very few of these deal with the *Fables,* however.

IV: Editions of Greek and Latin Fable Collections

1. Chambry, Émile. *Ésope: Fables.* Paris: Société d'édition "Les belles lettres," 1927. Greek texts of 358 fables, with an Introduction, notes, and translations in French.

2. Ellis, Robinson. *The Fables of Avianus: with Prolegomena, Critical Apparatus, Commentary, Excursus and Index* [all in English; texts of forty-two fables in Latin]. Hildesheim: Georg Olms Verlagsbuchhandlung, 1966.

3. Hausrath, August. *Corpus fabularum Aesopicarum.* Vol. I, fasc. 1 only, Lipsiae [Leipzig]: B. G. Teubner, 1956–.

4. Perry, Ben Edwin. *Babrius and Phaedrus.* London: W. Heinemann; Cambridge, Mass.: Harvard University Press, 1965. Greek texts of a Prologue and

143 fables in verse of Babrius and Latin texts of 95 fables in verse by Phaedrus, in five Books with Prologues and Epilogues. With comprehensive Introduction, notes and prose translations in English. Perry prints Perotti's Appendix to Phaedrus, containing 32 additional fables in Latin verse, and there is also an Appendix listing the contents of or paraphrasing 722 additional fables whose various manuscript sources are noted.

5. Thiele, Georg. *Der lateinische Äsop des Romulus und die Prosafassungen des Phädrus: Kritischer Text mit Kommentar und einleitenden Untersuchungen von Georg Thiele.* Heidelberg: Winter, 1910. Contains a lengthy introduction with discussions of the manuscript stemma, comparative Latin texts of ninety-eight fables with notes on variants, and a word list.

V: The Life of Aesop

1. Perry, Ben Edwin. *Aesopica*, Volume I. (A second volume was apparently intended, but was never published.) Urbana: University of Illinois Press, 1952. This volume includes texts of the two major Greek versions and one Latin version of the *Life of Aesop*, together with other materials, notes, and an extensive Introduction.

2.————. *Studies in the Text History of the Life and Fables of Aesop.* Haverford, Pennsylvania: American Philological Association, 1936.

English translations of all or part of the *Life of Aesop* have been published from time to time together with collections of the *Fables* in English. One such is:

3. Stern, Simon, ed. *The Life and Fables of Aesop: a selection from the version of Sir Roger l'Estrange.* New York: Taplinger, 1970.

VI: Critical and Scholarly Studies and Other Works of Related Interest

1. Aarne, Antti Amatus. *Die Tiere auf der Wanderschaft, eine Märchenstudie.* Hamina, Finland: Suomalaisen tiedeakatemian kustantama, 1913.

2. Barnett, Lionel D., ed. and rev. *Hitopadeśa. The Book of Wholesome Counsel*, tr. Francis Johnson. London: Chapman and Hall, Ltd., 1928.

3. Baum, Richard. *Recherches sur les oeuvres attribuées à Marie de France.* Heidelberg: C. Winter, 1968.

4. Feldmann, Susan, ed. *African Myths and Tales.* New York: Dell, 1963.

5. Gonzales, Ambrose E. *With Aesop along the Black Border.* The State Company: 1924. Rpt. New York: Negro University Press, 1969.

6. Hausrath, August. "Achiqar und Aesop: das Verhältnis der orientalischen zur griechischen Fabeldichtung," in *Sitzungsberichte der Heidelberger Akademie der Wissenschaften.* Heidelberg: C. Winter, 1918.

7. Holmes, Urban T., Jr. *A History of Old French Literature from the Origins to 1300.* Revised edition. New York: Russell and Russell, 1962.

8. Jauss, Hans Robert. *Untersuchungen zur mittelalterlichen Tierdichtung.* Tubingen: M. Niemeyer, 1959.

9. Keidel, George C. *A Manual of Aesopic Fable Literature; a first book of reference for the period ending A.D. 1500.* Baltimore: The Friedenwald Company, 1896. Rpt. New York: Burt Franklin, 1972.

10. Klingender, Francis. *Animals in Art and Thought to the End of the Middle Ages.* Cambridge, Mass.: The M.I.T. Press, 1971.

11. Kramer, S. N. *History Begins at Sumer.* Garden City, New York: Doubleday and Company, 1959.

12. Kuschel, Rolf. *Animal Stories from Bellona Island.* Gyldendal: National Museum of Denmark, 1975.

13. Lenaghan, R. T., ed. *Caxton's Aesop.* Cambridge, Mass.: Harvard University Press, 1967.

14. Mall, Eduard. *Zur Geschichte der mittelalterlichen Fabelliteratur.* Halle: Special Issue of "Zeitschrift für romanische Philologie," Vol. 9, No. 2/3, 1885.

15. Mickle, Emanuel J., Jr. *Marie de France.* New York: Twayne Publishers, Inc., 1974.

16. Warnke, Karl. *Die Quellen des Esope der Marie de France.* Halle: Niemeyer, 1900.

ABOUT THE AUTHORS

NORMAN R. SHAPIRO, professor of romance languages and literatures at Wesleyan University, is a leading translator of medieval and modern French. He earned his B.A., M.A., and Ph.D. in romance languages at Harvard University. His translations span a wide range of genres including French farces and novels, works by black French-speaking poets, and medieval fables and lore. He lives in Middletown, Connecticut.

HOWARD NEEDLER received a B.S. from Yale University, was a Rhodes scholar at Oxford, and received a Ph.D. in Italian literature at Columbia University. The author of *St. Francis and St. Dennis in the Divine Comedy* and numerous articles, he is professor of letters at Wesleyan University. His home is in New Haven.

ABOUT THE BOOK

FABLES FROM OLD FRENCH has been composed in Garamond with Solemnis titling by Heritage Printers, printed on Warren's Oldstyle and bound in Johanna Centennial by Halliday Lithograph.

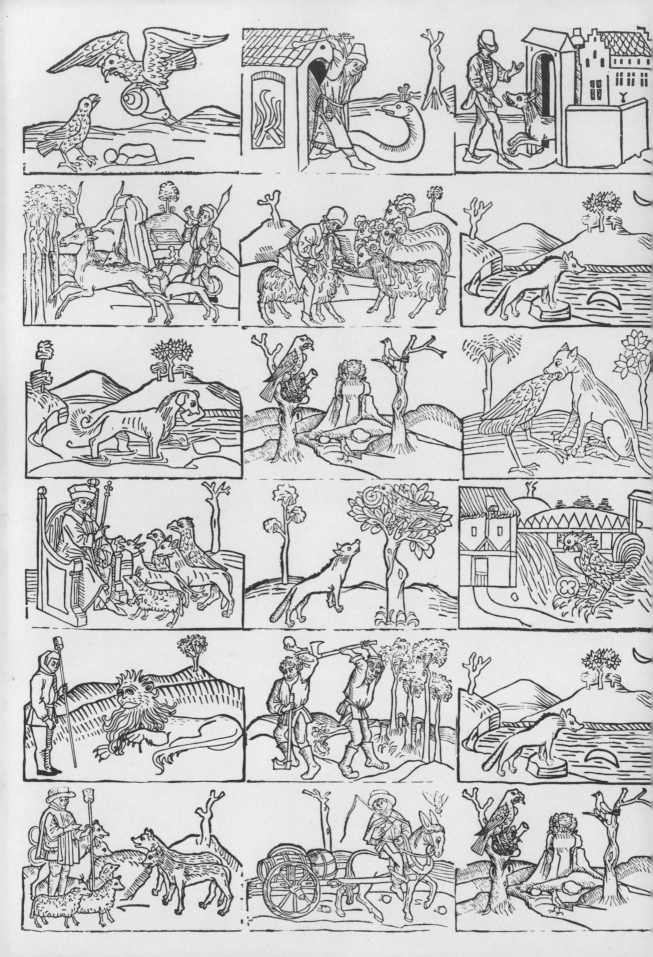